D0188835

Camp Club Girls

Alexis

AND THE
SACRAMENTO
SURPRISE

DISCARDED

Camp Club Girls

Alexis

AND THE
SACRAMENTO
SURPRISE

Erica Rodgers

BARBOUR
PUBLISHING

© 2010 by Barbour Publishing, Inc.

Editorial assistance by Jeanette Littleton.

ISBN 978-1-60260-270-0

All rights reserved. No part of this publication may be reproduced or transmitted for commercial purposes, except for brief quotations in printed reviews, without written permission of the publisher.

Churches and other noncommercial interests may reproduce portions of this book without the express written permission of Barbour Publishing, provided that the text does not exceed 500 words and that the text is not material quoted from another publisher. When reproducing text from this book, include the following credit line: "From *Alexis and the Sacramento Surprise,* published by Barbour Publishing, Inc. Used by permission."

Scripture taken from the HOLY BIBLE, NEW INTERNATIONAL VERSION®. NIV ®. Copyright © 1973, 1978, 1984 by International Bible Society. Used by permission of Zondervan. All rights reserved.

Cover design © Thinkpen Design

This book is a work of fiction. Names, characters, places, and incidents are either products of the author's imagination or used fictitiously. Any similarity to actual people, organizations, and/or events is purely coincidental.

Published by Barbour Publishing, Inc., P.O. Box 719, Uhrichsville, Ohio 44683, www.barbourbooks.com

Our mission is to publish and distribute inspirational products offering exceptional value and biblical encouragement to the masses.

Member of the
Evangelical Christian
Publishers Association

Printed in the United States of America.

Dickinson Press, Inc., Grand Rapids, MI; Print Code D10002179; February 2010

A Problem at the Park

SLAM!

Alexis Howell jolted up in bed. She sat for a moment while her shocked heart slowed down.

Who on earth is banging doors this early in the morning? she thought. *It's only—*

She looked at the clock on her wall.

"Nine thirty!" Alexis exclaimed.

She knew she had set her alarm for eight o'clock, but she reached over and saw that someone had unplugged it. Alexis threw the covers off and flew out of bed. Why did her little brothers always mess with her on important days? She didn't want to be late!

She yanked on a pair of shorts, slipped on a pair of flip-flops, and scurried toward the door. Alexis passed her desk and reached out, but her hand closed on thin air.

"Where's my paper?" she yelled.

"You mean this one?" her brother asked. He was standing at the top of the stairs waving a paper airplane.

The boys were twins, and at first glance she sometimes couldn't tell them apart, which made them even more annoying.

"You made it into an airplane?" cried Alexis. "Give it to me!"

"You should have said *please*," her brother said. He drew his arm back and flung the airplane down the stairs.

"No!" cried Alexis. She bounded toward the stairs.

She could see the important paper circling toward the living room. Here, like everywhere else in her house, were countless stacks of paper. Her mother and father were both lawyers. They worked in the same office, and since that office was being renovated, all of their work had migrated to the Howell house. If that tiny paper airplane landed in the middle of that mess, she would never find it!

Alexis leaped down the first three stairs. On the fourth, however, her foot landed on a remote-control race car and flew out from beneath her. Alexis crashed down the rest of the stairs and slammed into the closest pile of files. It was a paper explosion.

"What on earth?" cried Mrs. Howell. She ran in from the kitchen and found Alexis knee-deep in paper, searching. More paper still fell like rain from the ceiling.

"Oh no!" said Alexis. "Where is it? Where is it!"

"Calm down, Alexis," said Mrs. Howell. "Where is what?"

"The e-mails! I printed out Kate's e-mail and wrote her flight information on the back. If I can't find it, we won't know when to get her! And I'm running late!"

Her mom placed a hand on her shoulder.

"Calm down," she said. "We have plenty of time. Here, I'll help." Alexis's mom began stacking her files. In no time she uncovered a small, crumpled airplane. Alexis flattened it out and took a deep breath.

"Thanks, Mom." Alexis read the page again just to be sure it was the right paper airplane.

Camp Club Update
From: Alexis Howell

Hey girls! How is everyone? I'm great, but things have been boring since I got home from camp. I have two more weeks until cheerleading starts, so I'm at home with my brothers way too often! The only investigating I've done lately involves a missing Spiderman sock and the cat from next door. Isn't that sad?

Oh! I almost forgot! A lady at my church could use your prayers. Her name is Miss Maria, and she runs a nature park outside the city. It's a

*great place to see the local plants and animals,
but lately not many people have been visiting. If
Miss Maria can't get some big business she's going
to have to close the park. The park is all she has.
It would be awful if she had to sell it. She rented
some fake dinosaurs that look real and really
move, like the animals at Disneyland. Maybe this
will bring more business! Pray that it does!*

Kisses, Alex

Alex,

*It was so good to get your update! I'm sorry
to hear about Miss Maria. Is she really getting
mechanical dinosaurs? That is so awesome! Are
you up for a visitor? Sounds like you could use a
little excitement, and I can get there easily. My
grandpa is a pilot and gets me great deals to fly all
over the country. That really comes in handy when
I get the urge to visit California! LOL!*

*I would love to see you, and besides, I've never
seen animatronics that close up before! Do you
think Miss Maria would let me touch them? Let
me know what your mom says!*

Love, Kate

Alexis must have read Kate's e-mail forty-three times, but her heart was still racing. She had thought she wouldn't see any of the other Camp Club Girls until next summer, but in less than an hour Kate would be there! Alexis was sure this week would be amazing. How could it not be? They would find some crazy case to solve—maybe a stolen piece of art, or a break-in at the Governor's Mansion. Whatever they did would be ten times better than doing nothing—as she had done for the last month.

On her way to the kitchen Alexis poked her head into the bathroom to glance in the mirror. She pulled her loose brown curls into a quick ponytail and wiped the sleep from her eyes. They were an electric blue, and Alexis knew they clashed with her hair, but she liked being a little different.

She stepped back and scrunched her face. If only she could make her freckles disappear! They stood out on her pale skin like spots on a snow leopard, and she could never decide if she liked them or not. She had tried once to cover them with her mom's makeup, but it had been the wrong color, and waterproof so she couldn't remove it easily with water. She hadn't known that her mother had special make-up remover. That day she had gone to school looking like a pumpkin.

Oh well. Sometimes she was proud of her freckles. They measured how good her summer had been. The more fun she had in the sun, the darker they got.

"*Lots* of fun in the sun this year, I guess," she said, then she spun out of the bathroom. Her toasted blueberry waffles were waiting for her in the kitchen.

"Thanks, Mom," Alexis said as she ate.

"You're welcome, but do you really need to say it with your mouth full?"

Alexis swallowed. "Sorry."

Her twin brothers, who were seven, had freckles just like Alexis but had also inherited the red hair from her mother's side of the family. The boys finished eating and began playing hide-and-seek among the towering files in the living room. Alexis ignored the possibility of disaster and ate quickly. She was counting down the minutes until she would see Kate at the airport.

Twenty minutes until they left.

Forty minutes until they parked.

Forty-five minutes until—

The television caught her eye. She usually ignored the news, but the anchorwoman with big hair was showing a shot of her friend, Miss Maria, standing in front of the nature park. Alexis grabbed the remote and turned up the volume just in time to hear the introduction to the story.

"Let's go to Channel 13 reporter Thad Swotter for more about this story."

"Thank you, Nicky," said the newsman. He flashed the camera a cheesy smile. "Yesterday one more company refused to sponsor Aspen Heights Conservation Park. That makes them number 10 on the list of people who have denied the park money this year. You may ask, *Thad, who's counting?* And I would say no one—except the park's owner."

Thad Swotter laughed into the camera, his mouth still stretched into a wide, fake smile.

"As a last-ditch effort to revive the park," he continued, "Maria Santos has scattered a stampede of mechanical dinosaurs throughout the park. The exhibit opens to the public today and will be there through the end of this month."

"Well, Thad," said the woman with the big hair, "do you think this will bring in more visitors?"

"I know Miss Santos hopes so," said the reporter. "It looks like she's spent her life's savings on the project. It certainly is creative, but I think it will take more than a bunch of toy dinosaurs to keep that park from becoming extinct!"

"Thanks, Thad. Now over to Chris for last night's sports report."

Alexis had forgotten about her waffles. None of her friends had ever been on the news before, but she wasn't excited. She was worried. Had Miss Maria really spent the last of her savings on those dinosaurs? If so, things must be pretty bad.

Alexis whipped out her bright pink notebook and scribbled:

Mission: Find a way to help Miss Maria.

Step One: Visit park with Kate and ask how we can help.

Going to the park was a great idea. It seemed like the perfect place to find an adventure. Kate really wanted to see the dinosaurs, and maybe they could help Miss Maria while they were there. Alexis shoved her notebook into her pink camouflage backpack. She never left home without it. Taking notes was one of the most important things an investigator could do, and Alexis considered herself an investigator. After all, the Camp Club Girls were regularly finding cases to solve.

Half an hour later Alexis and her mom were at the airport, waiting for Kate to pop through the exit gate of the security checkpoint. Mrs. Howell said that she used to be able to meet people at the door of the plane. Alexis couldn't imagine that. For as long as she could remember she had waited for visitors here—next to the gift shop, and at a safe distance from the burly security guards. It would have been fun to meet Kate at her gate—they would already be having a blast. But Alexis was stuck waiting near a rack of overpriced California coffee mugs.

The first thing Alexis noticed was Kate's new pair of glasses flashing through the crowd. They were bright green and came to a point at the sides. They made Alexis think of the Riddler, one of the best Batman villains. She laughed at the thought and met her friend with a hug.

"It's so good to see you!" said Alexis. "How was your flight?"

"Long, and they wouldn't let Biscuit sit with me! He had to go *under the plane*! Do you have any idea how *cold* it gets down there?"

Alexis caught her breath and stopped abruptly. She'd forgotten about Biscuit! How many times when the boys begged for a dog had Mrs. Howell firmly told them their house, especially now, with all its stacks of paper, was no place for a dog! Alexis suspected the real issue was that her mom didn't like dogs. At all. She frowned when people walking their dogs didn't clean up their droppings in the yard. She'd also opposed a neighborhood park being turned into a dog park.

What will Mom do? Alexis thought. *Will she make Kate send Biscuit back home? Will she make Biscuit stay in the garage? But then Biscuit will cry all night.*

"Alexis!" Mrs. Howell called. Kate realized that her mother and friend were far ahead of her. She glanced at her mother's face. Mrs. Howell looked cheerful and friendly. Apparently she either hadn't heard Kate's words clearly or didn't know that Biscuit was a dog.

Lord, please help Mom be nice about Biscuit! Alexis prayed silently.

Alexis's mom led the girls to the baggage claim. They picked up a neat little suitcase and a not-so-neat black and white puppy. At the sight of Biscuit, Mrs. Howell's smile faltered.

"Don't worry, Mom," said Alexis. "Biscuit can stay in my room—away from your files." Mrs. Howell said that she wasn't worried, but her face relaxed only a bit. Alexis knew that she had been thinking of the endless stacks of paper that could easily become chew toys and chaos.

Thank You, God! Alexis mentally murmured. She knew if Mom didn't say anything now, she never would. Now, if only Alexis and Kate could make *sure* Biscuit didn't get in Mom's way or cause trouble!

"We're going straight to the park," Alexis said to Kate as they arrived at the family's green Durango. They buckled themselves into the back seat, and Mrs. Howell dug around in her purse for some cash to pay for parking.

"The dinosaur exhibit opens today, so tons of people should be there," Alexis added as her mom pulled onto the highway.

Alexis was wrong. A half-hour later Mrs. Howell drove through the two towering redwoods at the entrance to Aspen Heights and frowned. Theirs was only the second car in the parking lot.

"I don't understand!" said Alexis. "Where is everyone? It was on the news and everything!"

"Don't worry, sweetheart," said her mother. "I'm sure more people will come. It's not even lunchtime yet."

Lunchtime came and went, though, and only a handful of people were enjoying the park. Alexis and Kate walked the shade-speckled trails with Biscuit on his leash.

"Wow!" said Kate. "There are so many plants here!"

"I know," said Alexis. "Miss Maria tries to keep a little of everything. She especially likes the endangered ones."

"Oh look! Another dinosaur!" Kate ran up to a Triceratops that looked like it was eating the fuzzy leaves of a mule ear. A miniature Triceratops was feet away near an evergreen bush. Alexis figured it must be the baby.

Miss Marie had certainly arranged the dinosaurs well. Alexis and Kate had to look hard to see the electrical cords and power boxes hidden among the plants, feeding power to the animatrons.

15

Alexis had never been easily able to imagine what dinosaurs looked like. But these animatrons were full-sized. They had been meticulously fashioned to resemble the original animals as closely as possible. Alexis began to understand the fascination some people felt for the extinct creatures.

"They're a lot different than in the *Jurassic Park* movies," Alexis noted. "I thought they'd be taller than this. Some of them aren't too much bigger than a large man."

Kate laughed. "Alexis, you're the one from California! You should be the first to know that movies aren't always true to life!"

Alex grinned. "Actually, most of the movie stuff goes on around Los Angeles, and that's quite a ways down the coast. We see movie crews around shooting sometimes. But other than that, we don't have much more to do with the entertainment industry than you probably do in Philadelphia."

"Well, most of the dinosaurs were actually probably smaller than the ones in those movies. And sometimes the movies weren't accurate in re-creating the dinosaurs.

"Like these Velociraptors," Kate said, pointing at the herd of creatures with their waving arms. "See how they're kind of feathery looking? This is more accurate than the portrayals that show them with scaly, lizard-like skin.

Just a couple of years ago some paleontologists found a preserved Raptor forearm in Mongolia that proved it had feathers."

"How in the world do you know all that?" Alexis asked.

"Discovery Channel," Kate said with a grin. "And a teacher who spends her summer looking for dinosaur footprints!"

The girls walked along the pathway to the next creature, a dromaeosaurus lurking near a nest of eggs that looked like they came from a much larger beast.

"This one is even better than the Raptor!" said Kate. "Look! Its eyes blink!"

"Actually, Kate, I think it's *winking*! The other eye is stuck!"

The girls' laughter was cut short. They jumped in alarm as another dinosaur nearby, a Dilophosaurus, raised its head and bellowed. As the animatron swung its head around, Alex gasped.

"It spit at me!" she cried. "I've been assaulted by dinosaur spit! That must have sent out a gallon of water, and all on me! My shirt is soaked!"

Kate clutched her sides, laughing. "Well, at least they used water instead of adding more components to make the expectorant more realistic!"

"What?" Alexis asked.

"At least they didn't make it slimy and mucusy like real spit might have been!"

"Oh, I'm sorry I asked," Alex said. "Wait a minute while I throw up at that thought—and it wouldn't be water, either!"

The rest of the animatron trail passed uneventfully. More bellows and eye blinks and movements, but thankfully, no more assaults by spitting dinosaurs.

As Alex's shirt started to dry in the hot sun, the girls started giggling again about the spitting dinosaur.

"Sounds like a rock band," Alex said. "The Spitting Dinosaurs."

"Yeah, or maybe a little kids' T-ball team!" Kate added.

The girls laughed all the way back to the visitors' center. The entrance from the walking trails looked like an old log cabin with a green roof. That led into another larger building with the same log design. The larger building housed more exhibits and displays about nature and animals.

Alexis noticed that more cars were now in the parking lot, and her smile stretched even wider. It would be horrible if the dinosaurs turned out to be a waste of Miss Maria's money.

When they walked into the visitors' center, a lanky

teenager greeted them from behind the desk.

"Hey, Alex, who's your friend?" he called out.

"Hi, Jerry. This is Kate." Jerry was tall and a little thin, as if the summer between eighth and ninth grade had stretched him out. His dark hair had light streaks from spending plenty of time in the sun. Between that, his flip-flops, and his tan, he looked as if he'd stepped right out of a surfing movie.

"Hi, Kate," said Jerry. "It's good to meet you!"

"You, too," said Kate, looking at her shoes shyly.

Bam! The door to the visitors' center flew open and Miss Maria stormed in.

"That newsman from Channel 13 just got here," she said. "Try to ignore him." She stopped to hug Alexis with her wiry, suntanned arms and shook hands with Kate.

"But Miss Maria," said Jerry, "don't you want to be on the news? It might get more people to come to the park."

"Yes, it might, but that young reporter isn't very pleasant." Miss Maria tucked a piece of short salt-and-pepper hair behind her ear. "More than toy dinosaurs, huh?"

Miss Maria grumbled to herself until a visitor stuck his head through the open door and called to her.

"Hey, Maria! Good job with the Triceratops and Raptor footprints. They're so realistic! And I'm glad you put a Raptor by the fountain. He looks good there. I'll be back with my family, and I'll encourage my students to come!"

Miss Maria thanked the man, who introduced himself as a biology professor from one of the local colleges. "But I've always longed to be a paleontologist!" he confessed.

As the professor waved good-bye, Alexis noticed that Miss Maria didn't look too happy.

"He liked the dinosaurs!" Alexis said. "What's wrong, Miss Maria? Didn't you hear? He's bringing his whole family! And he's sending his students over!"

Miss Maria looked out the window and tapped a finger on the sill.

"Yes, I heard him," said Miss Maria. "The question is, did *you*? He said he liked the footprints—what footprints is he talking about? Alexis, did you and your friend notice any footprints this morning?"

Alexis shook her head. "But we weren't looking that closely," she said.

"And there shouldn't be a Raptor near the fountain at all," said Maria. "I put them all in the dogwood grove."

"Someone must have moved him," said Alexis.

"But why would they do that?" asked Kate.

"Why would anyone dig up my pansies, or carve their initials in a hundred-year-old redwood tree?" said Maria.

"Sometimes they do it because they have no respect for God's creation. Sometimes they do it to cause trouble. And sometimes they do it to show off to their friends. Who knows why else they do it! But moving around some of those dinosaurs isn't easy, and they're liable to mess up the wires—to even get electrocuted. Let's go take a look."

Miss Maria had placed the six Raptors together in a little herd. Sure enough, when they rounded the corner to the dogwood grove, the smallest one was missing. Little footprints led away through the trees. They had three toes, like a bird had made them, with two of the toes being longer than the third. The group followed the tracks along the trail until they reached the fountain. Then they saw him.

The diminutive dinosaur was posed on the edge of the fountain. Fortunately, he was one of the models that wasn't animated or electric. He was about two feet tall and bright green. His long tail kept him balanced on his back legs as he leaned toward the water. He looked as if he'd simply left the herd to get a drink.

"Weird!" said Jerry.

"Yeah," Alexis agreed.

She walked carefully around the fountain. She and Alexis had been laughing too hard earlier to notice the footprints if they'd been there. And this Raptor hadn't stood out when they'd seen it earlier—they didn't know Miss Maria hadn't put it by the water. Her mind kicked into overdrive just like it always did when she found something strange or out of place.

How did he get there? She wondered. *If someone moved him, why are there only dinosaur footprints in the mud? Shouldn't there be human prints, too?* Alexis pulled her notebook out of her backpack and instinctively began writing things down.

"Interesting, *and* irritating," said Miss Maria. She scooped up the Raptor and walked back toward the path holding him beneath her elbow. "You all go back to the visitors' center to greet people as they arrive," she said. "I'm going to go check around."

When they reached the center, Jerry's younger sister, Megan Smith, ran out to greet them. She was going into the seventh grade, like Alexis, and looked just like her brother, only with longer hair.

"Hi, guys!" Megan said. She pointed toward the parking lot. "Did you see the news crew?"

"Yeah," said Alexis.

"Maria wants us to stay away from them," said Jerry. Was Alexis imagining it, or was Jerry irritated?

"Oops. . . ," said Megan. "I gave the guy with the funny

hair a tour. He said he was interested in seeing all of the dinosaurs."

"That's okay, Meg," said Alexis. "A tour couldn't have done any harm. Maybe he liked the park enough to do a big story for the evening news."

Kate pushed her glasses up on the bridge of her nose and pointed toward the parking lot.

"I wonder why he's coming back," she said.

Sure enough, the reporter was striding across the parking lot. The wind tossed his bright blue tie around and lifted his hair up at an odd angle. Alexis wondered if he was wearing a wig. She would have thought he was too young for that, but then again, she also knew teachers and men at church who were way younger than her dad and hardly had any hair.

"Hi, kids!" he said. "I'm Thad. Thad Swotter— investigative reporter for Channel 13."

Not quite as impressive as he is on TV, thought Alexis.

"Some place you guys have here," Swotter said, looking around. His tone reminded Alexis of how her father greeted her great-aunt Gertrude. They visited her in Phoenix sometimes for Thanksgiving. He always *said* he was glad to be there, but Alexis didn't think he meant it.

"Miss Maria has worked very hard to share California's indigenous plants with our community," said Alexis. Thad Swotter smiled, and Alexis thought his perfect teeth might be a little big for his mouth.

"Indigenous, huh?" said Swotter. "That's quite a big word for such a little girl. You know, I was sure I saw some specimens that were *definitely* not native to California."

"Well, yes," said Megan. "On the tour I showed you the olive and the fig tree. Miss Maria works very hard to keep those alive through the winter. She likes to give people glimpses of other parts of the country, and even the world, too."

"Yes, I remember," said Swotter. "And the thorns were creepy. I'm glad we don't really have those in the foothills of the Sierra Nevada Mountains!"

"Thorns?" asked Kate.

"Yes," said Alexis. "Miss Maria's favorite plant is the Christ's-thorn in her greenhouse. It's planted next to a replica of the crown of thorns Jesus wore."

"Cool!"

"*Cool* it may be," said the reporter. "But I don't see how those thorns have anything to do with us. They're out of place."

"That's not true," said Megan. "God created all of it, so everything belongs."

"*God* created?" Swotter lifted his eyebrows in

amusement. "You kids are almost as bad as the bat that runs this place!"

Alexis reared up, ready to defend Miss Maria, but she took a deep breath instead. She knew it would be disrespectful to argue with Mr. Swotter. She even resisted the urge to roll her eyes—which was not easy when she was annoyed.

"This is exactly why nobody comes here!" Swotter laughed. "No one wants to come to a park to get preached at!"

"No one's preaching, sir," said Jerry respectfully. "People don't have to believe in God or Jesus to appreciate the plants. If it really bothers them, they can stick to the other parts of the park."

"They could," said Swotter, "but it'd be easier for them not to come at all. Look, kids, California has enough theme parks. If I want to hear a fairy tale, I'll go to Disneyland." He snickered again and walked off to examine a clump of poppies.

"He's rude," said Kate. "Good thing he doesn't act that rude on TV."

"He practically does," said Alexis. She looked around the empty park entrance. Where was Miss Maria? She had been gone for a long time.

"Those footprints were weird, weren't they?" Jerry

laughed. "It's like the dinosaurs just woke up and decided to explore the park!"

Thad Swotter stood up and scribbled furiously in his notebook. He headed toward his van, almost stomping on the poppies as he went. Alexis heard him yell something at his cameraman, who had fallen asleep on the steering wheel.

"What's up with him?" asked Megan.

"Maybe he's late," said Alexis. The group turned back toward the visitors' center. "I think we should check on Miss Maria." Before anyone could agree with her, a scream ripped through the trees.

Then all was silent.

"It came from over there." Jerry pointed toward the trail that led to the Triceratops.

"Oh no! Miss Maria!" Alexis tore off through the trees and the others followed.

When they came around the last corner, Alexis almost screamed herself. Miss Maria was lying on her back in the mud, next to the mother Triceratops. She wasn't moving.

Her large eyes stared unblinking into the cloudless sky.

The Footprints

Hospitals had never bothered Alexis. Her grandma was a nurse, so she had grown up visiting them. But this—this was different. Alexis had never visited someone who was actually *hurt*. She hated to admit it, but she was more than a little scared.

For the first time, Alexis noticed the smells of a hospital. Grandma's strong perfume had apparently masked all the hospital odors the other times she'd been in them. Alexis noticed that the hospital smelled like a mixture of cafeteria food and cleaning supplies.

Kate reached over and looped her arm through Alexis's.

"Don't worry," she said. "It could have been a lot worse."

Alexis tried to smile, but it didn't quite work.

Miss Maria was in a room on the fourth floor. The door was slightly open, and Alexis and Kate stopped just outside. A deep male voice drifted out into the hall.

Apparently a doctor was talking to her.

"Your back's not broken, Miss Santos, but you pulled some muscles pretty bad. If you're not careful, you could end up in a brace for months. I'd like to keep you here for observation. If everything goes well, you can go home in a couple of days."

"Thank you, Doctor," said Miss Maria. The strength in her voice calmed Alexis a little bit. Alex's racing heart slowed. The doctor swept out into the hallway, nearly knocking into the girls. Alexis heard the *click, click* of high heels behind her and turned to see her mom.

"That parking garage is a nightmare! Be glad I dropped you girls off at the doors!" She stepped forward and knocked lightly on the door. "Miss Maria?"

"Oh! Visitors!" chimed the older woman.

The girls filed into the room and sat down in the mauve chairs next to Miss Maria's white bed. She looked cheerful. Her mood was contagious, and Alexis smiled.

"How are you feeling?" she asked.

"Oh, just fine," said Miss Maria. "It doesn't hurt too badly right now."

They talked for a while, mostly about Miss Maria's injury and the attractive male nurse who kept coming in to check on her. Apparently Miss Maria had climbed up onto the Triceratops to get a better look at the footprints that were also leading from it to the distance. When it moved unexpectedly, she fell off.

"Serves me right for thinking I needed a bird's-eye view!" she said.

After twenty minutes, Mrs. Howell's phone rang. She dug it out of her purse and stepped outside to take the call. Her irritated voice drifted through the closing door. "No, Amanda, they don't owe anything. I told you that case was pro bono. . . . Yes. . .the hearing is next Friday. . . ."

After the door was shut, Miss Maria smiled conspiratorially. She crooked her finger and beckoned Alexis and Kate to come closer.

"Just grab a seat on the bed here," she said, patting the blanket on either side of her skinny legs. "I have a favor to ask."

Alexis sat down. She knew Miss Maria would need help now that her back was hurt. She probably wanted someone to feed her cat while she was in the hospital.

"It's about the park," Miss Maria said. "The doctor says I can't work for a while. I was wondering if you might be able to help me out a little." Alexis was puzzled. Why was Miss Maria whispering? It wasn't really a secret that the park would need a few extra hands, was it?

"Of course we'll help at the park, Miss Maria," said Alexis.

29

"Yeah," said Kate. "We can do whatever you need. It will be fun to see more of the dinosaurs."

"Well, that's just it. I hope you'll see a *lot* more of the dinosaurs," said Miss Maria. Her mouth stretched into a secret smile and she leaned toward them, wincing as her back was strained.

"My friend Gretchen told me that you found her kitten, Poncho, when no one else could. And your mother has mentioned the mysteries that you girls have already worked on. I would love the Camp Club Girls to investigate."

The word *investigate* made Alexis's heart race. She was really interested in the footprints and the little Raptor, but she also didn't want to make something out of nothing. Just the other day her father had accused her of seeing a mystery in everything. He had been joking, but she knew there was truth in what he said.

For instance, every time she went to the grocery store with her mother she couldn't help but ask herself crazy questions. Why could you pull an apple from the bottom of a pyramid without the others rolling to the floor? Why did Fred, the baker, constantly move the cakes around in his display case?

"I want you to find out what is happening," Maria said. Alexis turned her attention back to the hospital bed.

"Find out where those footprints are coming from, and how the dinosaur got from one place to the other. I don't like the idea of someone fiddling around in my park. If those dinosaurs are ruined, I'll have to pay for them. And if a visitor gets hurt, I could never forgive myself. Could I bother you girls with this?"

"Bother us? Miss Maria, it wouldn't bother us at all!" said Alexis.

"Really!" said Kate. "This is what we do best."

"Good," said Miss Maria. She sighed and slumped back in her bed. "It feels good to leave this in the hands of detectives I can trust. The police would just laugh at me."

Alexis dug out her notebook.

"Miss Maria, do you feel well enough to answer a few questions?" she asked. Alexis wanted to start the investigation right away. It felt like so long since she had helped someone. Miss Maria nodded, and Alexis launched her first question.

"When was the last time you visited the Triceratops and the Raptor? Before this afternoon, I mean."

"Last night as I closed the park," said Miss Maria. "I always walk a complete loop after I close the gates."

"And did everything seem normal?" asked Kate.

"Yes. Everything was just as I left it. I don't think anyone could have been hanging around and changed

3 CITIES PUBLIC LIBRARY
BOX 60
PARADISE VALLEY, AB
T0B 3R0

things after I left. I'm pretty sure no stragglers were there at the time. Not many people had been there in the first place. I paid extra close attention, since the dinosaur exhibit was opening today. I wanted everything to be perfect."

Alexis scribbled onto her paper.

"And do you recall seeing the footprints then?" she asked.

"No, I do not. But it was getting dark, so I could have overlooked them. I know the park like the back of my hand, so I never take a flashlight. It only attracts the bugs, and I must be sweet, because they bite me like crazy."

Mrs. Howell stuck her head back into the room. Her cell phone was still attached to her ear.

"Hey girls, I think we should let Miss Maria get some rest," she said.

The girls each grabbed a sun-wrinkled hand and squeezed.

"Get better," said Alexis. "And don't worry about a thing. The Camp Club Girls have this covered."

●—●—●

The girls went swimming in the neighborhood pool the next morning. Then promptly at 1:00 they sat at the Howells' computer. Earlier, Kate had texted the Camp

Club Girls who were available to meet them online for chat at 1 p.m. California time.

Promptly at 1:00, Alexis started the computer, while Kate pulled open her tiny battery-run notebook computer. "This is a new prototype one of my dad's students is working on for Dell," she explained. "Dad let me bring it as long as I'm careful. He even thought a road trial might be good for it," Kate explained. "It's even waterproof and is the smallest in existence."

"Wow!" Alexis exclaimed. "It must be cool to have a dad who works with technology!"

"Well, it can't do everything a full-sized computer can do," Kate admitted. "But it can handle more functions than an iPhone."

A subdued *ding* let the girls know a message was waiting.

Elizabeth: *Hey y'all. How are things in sunny Calif? I hear we have a new mystery on our hands.*

McKenzie: *I don't think I've recovered from the last mystery yet! Can this one beat our missing horse problem? Any more animals involved?*

Kate: *None so far. Unless you count Biscuit. . . who's here and is barking that he loves you.*

Biscuit yipped as if he could read the girls' notes!

Alexis: *But we are dealing with animatronics.*

Elizabeth: *What in the world are those?*

Kate: *Animated dinosaurs. They're built to be the size of real dinosaurs, and are electronically wired to show the mannerisms of real dinosaurs. Almost like movie props.*

Bailey: *Movie props? What are you guys involved in? Wish I could be there. I'd love to be in movies.*

Alexis: *Not movies! At a local park.*

Sydney: *They had those at a park in Virginia once when my aunt was filling in there for the park ranger department. They're cool.*

Bailey: *Sounds like a good movie to me. We'll call you Queen of the Dinosaurs, Alex. Maybe one will chase you up a tree.*

Alexis: *Just like that lady in* King Kong *got chased up a building, right?*

Bailey: *Something like that.*

Kate: *Anyway. . .no movies involved, Bailey. But there is a news anchor who's a real dog.*

Sydney: *I hope you're covering Biscuit's ears.*

Kate: *Oops, no offense Biscuit!*

Alexis: *Well, here's what's happening. . . .*

Alex filled the girls in on what was going on so far.

Elizabeth: *So if Miss Maria saw everything right, the park was perfectly normal when it closed. So whatever happened occurred after dark, but before lunchtime yesterday when you were there.*

Kate: *Right.*

Sydney: *Did you see anything strange in the park?*

Alex: *Well, at the fountain I noticed that there was only one set of footprints. Just those tiny Raptor ones. If a person had moved him, shouldn't there have been human prints, too? Boots or shoes or something?*

McKenzie: *But wouldn't there be a lot of ways someone could erase tracks? Sometimes when I'm out in the woods on my horse, even in the mud we don't leave tracks because the wind will blow leaves over the tracks.*

Sydney: *Or could someone have put down leaves or grass to start with so they wouldn't leave tracks?*

Bailey: *They could have even used stilts or*

something so they didn't leave prints. Did you see any holes in the ground?

Alex: *I guess those things could have happened. I think if they had stilts that would have been too noticeable; you know, their bringing them into the center and taking them out.*

McKenzie: *Perhaps the first thing we need to do is figure out the motive. Why would anyone move the dinosaurs or decorate the park with footprints?*

Bailey: *Do you think someone is just trying to be mean? Do people dislike Miss Maria?*

Alex: *I think everyone likes her but the rude news anchor. Everyone at church loves Miss Maria. And if someone was hanging around the park bothering her, Jerry would have told us.*

Elizabeth: *Didn't you say Miss Maria has some Christian stuff in the park? Maybe someone doesn't like that.*

Kate: *Alex and I wonder if it's a joke.*

Alexis: *After all, most kids would think it would be pretty funny to move a lady's dinosaurs around and make them come to life!*

Kate: *Of course they might get electrocuted in the process!*

McKenzie: *You know the area, Alex. Any bored kids around who might do this?*

Alex: *Thousands. Especially after that news anchor's rude report. They might do it thinking it's a joke, not to hurt Miss Maria.*

Kate: *By the way, I'll send you the link to the news story. The local channel has a video of it on their website.*

Elizabeth: *What's the plan of action?*

Alex: *We need more information. We'll have to investigate the scenes—the fountain and the Triceratops area.*

After a little bit more chat, the girls signed off.

"We can look harder for clues and do some interviews," Kate reassured Alex. "Maybe someone saw something."

"Yeah. Jerry and Megan live just outside the park, near Miss Maria. They might have noticed someone suspicious sneaking around," Alexis said.

●—●—●

At the dinner table that night, Alexis's thoughts turned to Miss Maria's money problems. How could the park raise enough to stay open? She prodded her family for ideas, but no one thought of anything original.

"She should charge a small fee to get in," said Mr. Howell.

"She does, but it's certainly not enough to cover all the bills, Rich," said Mrs. Howell as she dished salad onto the plates. "And I know she hates doing that. I told her before that she should raise the rates, but she won't agree to that."

"I hate this stuff!" said one of the twins, poking at his salad.

"Yeah! We're not rabbits!" said the other. But they both wolfed down the food in seconds.

"Mom's right," said Alexis, ignoring her brothers. "Miss Maria would never make people pay."

"What about extra donations?" asked Kate. "Would she accept gifts from people who *wanted* to give?"

"Kate, that's it!" said Alexis. "We could put a box at the entrance for donations. If visitors want to help, they can!"

"Oooh!" said one of the twins. "Put one by the bathroom and make people pay for their toilet paper!"

Mr. Howell was caught off guard. He burst out laughing, and a piece of lettuce flapped out of his mouth and onto his chin. Mrs. Howell shot a killer glance at the boys and then at her husband. The twins piled mashed potatoes onto their plates in silence. Alexis had a feeling that her dad sometimes got into more trouble than her brothers.

"Mom," said Alexis quietly, "can we turn on the TV?"

"You know I hate having that thing on while we eat," Mrs. Howell said. She put the chicken on the table and dashed off to get the rolls out of the oven.

"I know," Alexis called after her, "but there's supposed to be another story about the park!"

"Okay, but just for a few minutes."

Alexis got the remote off the TV and pressed a button. Thad Swotter's face appeared on the screen. His neon purple tie with blue stripes clashed horribly with his yellow hair.

"The reopening of Aspen Heights today was shrouded in mystery," the reporter said. "Maria Santos put mechanical dinosaurs in her nature park to draw in visitors. But it seems that the animatrons have begun wreaking havoc instead."

A picture of the Triceratops jumped onto the screen. The scene clipped away to show footprints. Swotter's voice broke in to explain.

"It seems that these footprints were not part of the original display. They just appeared. In fact, Maria Santos was injured today while inspecting them. Also, a small Raptor was found this afternoon a long way from his herd."

Now a picture of the fountain sprang onto the screen.

"He was found here, at the edge of the water, taking a drink. One park volunteer said that the dinosaurs may have simply come to life. I laughed at first, but that was before my camera captured *this.*"

Another series of pictures ran across the television. Dinosaurs and footprints were scattered all over the park, where none had been earlier. All the small, non-mechanical Raptors were huddled around the entrance sign, as if they were reading it. The baby Triceratops was in the middle of the bridge that crossed the creek. But the last picture was the scariest one of all: Tyrannosaurus Rex tracks. They led to the outer fence and back, as if the giant carnivore had been looking for a way out of the park.

"This is *way* too science fiction," said Alexis. She jumped out of her chair and ran to the phone.

"Alexis, please finish your dinner," said her mother as Alex dialed. Alexis held up a finger and begged silently for "just one minute." The phone on the other end of the line began to ring.

"Hello?" said a voice.

"Jerry! Are you watching this?" said Alexis.

"The news? Yeah! Isn't it cool?"

"It's crazy!" said Alexis. "Why didn't you tell me the dinosaurs had moved again?"

"How was I supposed to know?" said Jerry. "We closed the park after Miss Maria got hurt. I walked around the park before I closed it to make sure no stragglers were still in it. Everything was fine then. Then Megan and I cleaned the concession stand. I sure didn't hear or see anything. Miss Maria called a little later, asking us to let the news crew in to film some shots. I didn't stay with them; I had paperwork to do."

"Okay," said Alexis. "I was just shocked, that's all. I guess I'll see you tomorrow."

Alexis hung up the phone and crossed her arms. On the television, Thad Swotter was still rambling about dinosaurs coming to life.

"I don't know what's going on," Alexis explained as she sat back down at the table. "Jerry practically lives at the park and didn't know about the dinosaurs moving again. So how did the *reporter* know?"

"Yeah, Thad Swotter doesn't even like the park, so it's not like he'll hang around there for hours waiting for something to happen," Kate added.

"Wait!" Alexis exclaimed. "Thad Swotter doesn't like the park!"

Kate's eyes widened.

"How did he know the dinosaurs had moved again?"

she murmured. "Wasn't the park already closed?"

"Yeah," said Alexis. "It had been closed for hours." She leaned forward and quietly continued, "He knew because he was there, Kate. I bet he took the pictures after he moved the dinosaurs *himself*!"

The girls watched the screen as the camera zoomed in. Thad Swotter's goofy grin was more than a little suspicious. He was enjoying Miss Maria's troubles way too much.

"Enjoy it while you can, Mr. Swotter," Alexis said. "The Camp Club Girls are on to you now."

Jurassic Jaws

TO: Camp Club Girls
SUBJECT: Mystery Suspect

Suspect: Thad Swotter

Possible Motives: 1. Dislike of the park and Miss Maria. (He called her a "bat" yesterday and complained about the plants related to Christian history.)

2. Just to get a story—he is a young reporter who wants to be the best. A huge story, like dinosaurs coming to life, would give him quite a boost.

Evidence: Dinosaur positions found changed after news crew had been there.

Alexis hit the SEND key on her e-mail and picked up Biscuit's leash. She would take him for a walk around the block while Kate was getting dressed. It would give her some quiet time away from her little brothers.

Alexis stepped outside and stood on the front porch for

a moment, breathing in the dewy Sacramento morning.

Her cell phone suddenly buzzed with a text.

HI! BETH HERE. YOU'RE UP EARLY. GOT YOUR E-MAIL.

Alexis: LUV THIS TIME OF DAY. REMINDS ME THAT EVERY DAY IS A NEW BEGINNING. NO MTR HOW BAD ONE DAY IS, THE NEXT IS ALWAYS NEW AND DIFF.

Elizabeth: MAYBE THAT'S WHAT GOD MEANS WHEN HE SAYS HIS MERCIES ARE NEW EVERY MORNING. READ LAMENTATIONS 3:22-23. CUL8R.

Alexis stumbled as Biscuit pulled her onto the sidewalk.

"Okay, I'm coming! Want to help me figure out this case while you're sniffing around?" Biscuit looked back at her, as if puzzled. Then he dove headfirst into a clump of orange honeysuckle.

"Gotta tell you, Biscuit," said Alexis. "I think you're letting the Camp Club Girls down!"

Alexis thought about the mystery. She knew they could connect Thad Swotter to the mysterious movements of the dinosaurs. The question was, *how*?

At first it sounded strange. Why would a grown man resort to such silly tricks? Was Swotter just playing a joke on Miss Maria?

Possibly, but if he was, he was going to a lot of work just to annoy someone he barely knew. The second motive made more sense. If Swotter was the only reporter able to get pictures of the dinosaurs, it might give him a boost at his job. He *had* been sent to cover the opening of the dinosaur exhibit. While this was a big deal for Miss Maria, Alexis knew that a couple of robots at a nature park weren't really big news in California's capital.

In fact, Alexis couldn't remember seeing Thad Swotter before yesterday. He was probably the new guy—the new guy who wanted to make it to the top as fast as he could.

That reminded Alexis of a movie she had seen. The main character was a reporter who had to cover the worst stories ever, like cat fashion shows. Maybe Thad Swotter was like that guy and wanted a more dramatic story. Maybe he wanted one so much, he was making it happen.

Too bad he's not as funny as the guy in the movie, thought Alexis.

Would it really be that bad if Swotter wanted a good story? Alexis didn't think so, but moving the dinosaurs around did more than draw attention—it put people at risk. Miss Maria said between the weight of the dinosaurs and the sensitivity of their electrical setup—the hidden generators—someone could get hurt tampering with them.

Not only that, but if one of the *dinosaurs* got damaged, Maria would have to pay for it. That would be expensive, and Maria certainly couldn't handle an expense like that.

Thad Swotter must be using the park to catapult his way into stardom, no matter what it costs anyone else, Alex thought.

Alexis Howell was not about to let him succeed. She started jogging back to the house to discuss her thoughts with Kate.

●—●—●

After breakfast Mrs. Howell dropped the girls off at the park. It looked like a completely different place. The little Raptors were still huddled around the entry sign, but that was not what made Alexis gasp. The parking lot was *full*.

Hundreds of people were entering the park. After five minutes of pushing through the crowd, Alexis and Kate found Elena Smith, the woman who helped Miss Maria run the park. She was also Jerry and Megan's mother. In her late thirties, she had a wonderful sense of humor. The thick, dark hair that usually fell to the middle of her back was pulled up in a ponytail.

"Wow, Mrs. Smith!" called Alexis. "This must be a record! I've never seen so many people here before!" But Mrs. Smith looked anything but happy.

"This is crazy! Only three of us are here to answer

questions! We ran out of maps fifteen minutes after opening, too. Megan is inside making black and white copies to hand out."

"But this is good, right?" asked Kate. "More visitors are what Miss Maria needed, right?"

"Yes," said Mrs. Smith, "but not like this. These people don't really care about the park. They only want to see the dinosaurs that 'come to life.' Hey!" Mrs. Smith yelled over the crowd to a pair of girls who had left the path. "You're not allowed to walk over there!"

"We're not walking!" one of the teens answered. "We're *skipping*!" And they were. They were skipping right through the Jeffrey Pine saplings that had been planted by the church preschool class.

"You see?" said Mrs. Smith. "This has been happening all morning. Don't they realize they could kill those trees? They're delicate!" Mrs. Smith stomped off to make sure the trees were okay.

Alexis and Kate turned toward the visitors' center. Jerry met them in the doorway.

"Did you get up early?" asked Alexis. She noticed that Jerry's eyes were all red and puffy. He didn't answer her question.

"Isn't this great!?" he said, pointing to the teeming crowd.

"I don't know," said Alex. "It seems a little out of control." A tangle of loud kids rushed by, knocking into her without excusing themselves.

"Yeah," said Megan. "But we'll fix that." She handed Alex, Kate, and Jerry each a stack of maps.

"We're going to start giving guided tours!" said Jerry. "We can each lead one. Some people will still wander around on their own, but this will help us spread out and keep an eye on things."

"That's a good idea," said Alexis. "Someone's already rearranging the park at night. The last thing we need is visitors doing the same thing during the day!"

Alexis and Kate paused near the entrance sign. The little herd of Raptors was examining it, rocking their heads back and forth as if the writing confused them.

"They're turned on!" said Alexis. "The Raptor that was moved yesterday wasn't plugged back in. It was just sitting on the fountain."

Kate found the cord that powered the Raptors and followed it across the path to a large bush. A deep *humm hummm* came from behind its leaves.

"It's a generator!" Kate said. She ran back to where Alexis stood near the sign. "Not only did the suspect move the dinosaurs, he moved the generator, too. Then he plugged them back in!"

Whoever did this had put a lot of effort into it. Generators were heavy, Alexis knew, but a full-grown man—or reporter—would have been able to do it easily.

Alexis examined the dinosaurs one more time.

"These do look pretty funny," she admitted to Kate.

"Yeah, they're cute, standing and reading the park rules," Kate admitted. "Whoever did it has a sense of humor. But look at this ground!"

Kate pointed to the trampled grass. "I was hoping we'd find some clues."

"You're right. We'll never be able to find clues around here," Alex said, thinking of the hundreds of hiking boots, sneakers, and flip-flops that had already passed through that morning. "Maybe we'll have more luck inside."

"Come on, time for the tours!" Jerry announced.

Jerry directed a large group of people to Alexis. Alex's group took off ahead of Kate's group and led the visitors through the park. She pointed out interesting features but otherwise let them explore on their own. The most important thing was to make sure no one left the path. Already a first grader had fallen into a bed of California thistle. A few of the green barbs were still visible in the seat of her khaki Bermuda shorts as the group continued.

Alexis was excited. Guiding a tour group was the

perfect way to investigate the mystery sites. She could poke around and no one would even suspect that she was gathering evidence. It would just look like she was examining the plants.

When they reached the stream, the group had to wriggle its way around the baby Triceratops. The small dinosaur was still standing in the middle of the bridge, just as it had been shown on the news the night before. A science teacher from the local middle school reached out to touch him.

"Wow," he said. "It feels so real!"

"Please don't touch him, Mr. Bell," said Alexis politely. "I think they're very expensive and very delicate."

"Sure, Alexis. He's amazing! I could almost believe the rumors that the dinosaurs come to life! May I take a picture?"

"Of course," said Alexis. "Take as many as you want."

The crowd moved ahead to study the wildflower meadow, but Alexis lingered to look for clues on the bridge.

Nothing. Alexis knew she shouldn't be surprised. Hundreds of visitors were trampling this area, just as they'd done at the entrance. The suspect could have left absolutely anything and she would never know.

Alexis guided her group farther down the trail. At least she could still study the Tyrannosaurus Rex. His area was more secluded than the busy foot bridge.

Alex knew that it had taken ten people and one huge crane to place the Tyrannosaurus Rex among the aspens and dogwoods on the other side of the meadow. The slender trunks of the trees made him seem taller than his thirty feet. Alexis knew that although the Tyrannosaurus Rex didn't weigh anywhere near what a real Tyrannosaurus Rex would weigh, it was still well over a thousand pounds. There was no way Thad Swotter, or any other human, would be able to move this guy.

While the crowd stared at the mammoth creature, Alexis found the footprints that had been on the news. They were huge. She could even see the marks where the six-inch claws had scarred the earth.

She followed the tracks about a hundred yards. She looked back now and then to make sure no one from the group followed her. The footprints went all the way to the outer edge of Aspen Heights, where a chain-link fence marked the end of Miss Maria's property. Alexis gasped.

A hole gaped in the middle of the fence, right where the footprints ended.

"What could have done that?" she whispered. Fence cutters? Maybe, but how hard was it to break through metal? It must have taken a lot of strength.

Alexis was supposed to follow the evidence, but now

the evidence was starting to scare her. She saw no trace of humans here, either—just dinosaur footprints and a fence that looked as if a pair of Jurassic jaws had torn right through it.

Impossible. She refused to believe that the dinosaurs were actually coming to life.

Alexis heard someone call her name. It sounded like Mr. Bell. The tour was probably ready to move on.

"Coming!" she cried, and she weaved her way back through the trees.

At the Tyrannosaurus Rex, the group was busy taking pictures of the dinosaur staged so beautifully among the aspen trees. Alexis saw that Kate's group had caught up and was milling around the glade as well. One visitor was taking a video of the Tyrannosaurus Rex with his cell phone.

Alexis edged toward the dinosaur, just in case any clues were hiding in its monstrous shadow.

The dinosaur stood on its strong back legs. Its thighs were as thick as redwood trunks. Its arms, on the other hand, were tiny—hardly long enough to allow the creature to grasp his own hands. Alexis wondered if God might have given the Tyrannosaurus Rex monstrous teeth so the other dinosaurs wouldn't laugh at his silly proportions.

His head moved proudly through the air, looking over the forest and their little tour. Alexis knew a hidden generator hummed, although the noise of the tourists masked its gentle noise.

Kate joined Alex and started snapping pictures. "As soon as this tour is over, wait before you start the next one," Alex told Kate. "I have something to tell you!"

Kate gave Alexis a searching look. "Okay, sounds like you found a clue."

"Well, not a clue, but certainly something strange," Alex said. "But we don't have time to go into it now."

"Okay," Kate said, going back to her photography. "Stand by the Tyrannosaurus Rex and let me get a picture of you with it."

Alex got near the animatron and dodged the thick tail as it swung back and forth. Alexis was looking for clues as to where the footprints began when she heard a loud *crack* and an angry *roar*! She looked up and didn't have time to scream.

The Tyrannosaurus's head plummeted toward her, hundreds of sharp teeth gleaming in the sun.

The tour group fled the aspen grove, some screaming and some laughing. Children were scared out of their minds, crying and hiding their heads in their mother's necks. Needless to say, the tour was over.

"Did you see that?" called one girl to her friend. "It almost bit that girl's head off!"

Kate ran over to Alex. "Are you okay?"

Alex weakly nodded. She was still shaking.

"Come on. I think you need a Coke," Kate said. "You need to sit down inside the visitors' center and relax a minute."

Alexis and Kate were following the crowd back to the visitors' center at a slow walk. Alexis glanced back and saw the slumping dinosaur. He was bent over the spot where Alexis had been standing, and he wasn't moving anymore.

Alexis didn't think the Tyrannosaurus Rex had really attacked her, but she was shaken up. It was hard not to be scared when a head full of teeth came at you out of nowhere. On the other hand, it *wasn't* hard to imagine what the Channel 13 guy would say about the park tonight.

Alexis could already hear it. *"A young girl was attacked today by an animal that has been extinct for thousands of years. . . ."*

Alexis didn't notice when they crossed back over the bridge, but Kate grabbed her arm and spun her around.

"Alexis!" she whispered. "The baby Triceratops—it stuck its tongue out at me!"

"I guess its mother needs to teach it some manners," joked Alexis.

But Kate didn't laugh.

"Alexis, look at the power cord. . .it isn't plugged in."

Puzzling Pictures

The panic caused by the Tyrannosaurus Rex spread through the park faster than fire. At the end of the afternoon, Mrs. Smith and Megan pushed the gates closed. Jerry had already been on the phone with Miss Maria and had called an electrician who had helped set up the animatrons. Hopefully he could figure out what was wrong with the dinosaur.

Alexis and Kate decided to use the free afternoon to sleuth. They decided it wasn't enough to wait until something else happened. They had to get ahead and catch him in the act.

So now Alexis and Kate were dragging Jerry and Megan around the park with a handful of cameras.

"Hey, Alex," said Jerry. "Why are we doing this?"

"We're trying to find out how the dinosaurs are moving around at night," said Alexis.

"Why does it matter?" asked Megan. "They're bringing in a lot of business, aren't they? Why don't we just leave it alone?"

"Because Miss Maria says that moving them is dangerous. Someone could get hurt. And I know it sounds crazy, but if they really *are* coming to life. . . someone could get torn apart." The memory of a murderous mouth full of teeth flashed through Alexis's mind. She shivered.

"Yeah," said Kate. "People today get mad over a cold cup of coffee. What do you think they would do if their kid got eaten by a park display?"

Alexis laughed nervously. She knew that Kate was right. Last week one of her mom's clients wanted to sue a fast food restaurant because the ice in his drink melted too fast. Mrs. Howell had refused to pursue the lawsuit, of course, but it made Alexis think. The smallest, silliest things could make people so angry. A real dinosaur attack would make them furious.

The four kids walked past the entrance sign. The dinosaurs weren't there anymore since Mrs. Smith had taken them all back to the dogwood grove. Alexis was sure they wouldn't be at the entrance in the morning, but were they running all over the park by themselves? And what about the baby Triceratops? How had it stuck its tongue out without being plugged in?

What was really going on around here?

The four of them walked the entire park, looking for the best places to put the cameras. Kate stuck one near the Triceratops meadow. She crept along the edge of the grass, placed the camera on a rock, and ran all the way back to the trail. She kept glancing over her shoulder, as if she expected the Triceratops to charge any second. Alexis couldn't blame her.

Next they put cameras where the dinosaurs had been found out of place—near the fountain and the entrance sign.

"These things are tiny!" said Megan, leaning on the wall of the fountain and looking at one of the cameras. "Where's the film?"

"Film?" said Kate. "*Please.* These babies are digital."

"Where on earth did you get this many digital cameras?" said Jerry.

"My dad uses them at his work. These are the models from a couple years ago. They have bigger and better ones now. Actually, *smaller* and better." Kate snickered at her joke and led the group through the bushes and toward the Raptors.

"You're such a nerd!" Alexis teased. "What would I do without you?"

Kate smiled and bent down to place the last camera on the ground. She hid it in a clump of fuzzy mule ears.

The bright yellow flowers dusted pollen all over her arm. She adjusted the camera so the lens was watching the path to the visitors' center.

"There! It's done!" Alexis said triumphantly.

"So," said Jerry to Kate, "do those cameras just take a picture every five minutes or something?"

"No way," said Kate. "We could miss tons of stuff if we did it that way! I turned on the motion sensor. Anytime these little red lights sense something move, they'll snap a picture." Jerry pushed Megan playfully in front of the camera.

SNAP!

"It works!" he said.

"Of course it works!" said Kate. "And now I have a picture of your sister's ankle clogging my memory card!" Kate leaned down and hit the DELETE button.

"You're amazing, Kate," said Alexis. "I am so glad you came to visit! If it weren't for you, I'd be doing an all-night stakeout."

Megan giggled. "That's not my idea of a slumber party—spending the night in a park of dinosaurs that may or may not eat you!" she said.

"We'd better get back to the front. Mom will be here any time," Alexis said.

On their way back to the parking lot, Alexis stopped

to check the donations box. Mrs. Smith liked the idea and had helped her hang it up. It was a simple wooden box with a lock on the lid and a hole in the top so people could drop in additional donations. The small sign on it read, DONATIONS APPRECIATED! ALL FUNDS KEEP THE PARK BEAUTIFUL FOR YOUR ENJOYMENT! THANK YOU!

The box contained seventy-nine cents, three gum wrappers, and a check for fifteen dollars from Mr. Bell, the science teacher.

"Visitors weren't very generous today, were they?" asked Jerry.

"Mr. Bell was," said Alexis. "Did you expect a miracle?"

"Why not?" asked Megan.

"Huh?"

"Why not expect a miracle?" said Megan a little louder. "I've been praying for one a lot lately. I mean, if God could do all those cool things in the Bible, surely He can take some time to help Miss Maria."

"I think He is," said Kate. "She has us to help her while she's hurt. And it's probably only a matter of time before the money comes in."

"How can you be so sure?" asked Jerry.

Alexis wanted to answer him. She wanted to be like Elizabeth and break out a Bible verse that explained exactly why she trusted God to fix this mess, but she couldn't. She couldn't explain why she trusted so completely in something she couldn't see. Jerry believed in God—they went to the same church. But Alexis sensed that he had a hard time trusting anyone but himself.

"I'm not sure *how*," Alexis finally said, "but I know it will happen." She smiled at him, hoping it would make him feel better. He smiled back, but Alexis could tell that he wasn't convinced. Mrs. Howell's old red van pulled up to the curb.

"See you guys tomorrow!" Alexis and Kate called. As Alexis got in the car, she still wished she was better at explaining what was in her heart. Somehow she knew everything would work out.

There was no more investigating to do at the moment. The cameras would do their job, and hopefully the Camp Club Girls would have fresh evidence to go on in the morning.

While they waited for dinner, Alexis and Kate thought of a new way to help Miss Maria. They went to work on the computer designing a poster for the park and then sent a copy to the other Camp Club Girls. Bailey e-mailed back that it looked like a movie poster.

Alexis smiled. Alexis loved to look at the posters at the movie theaters. In the middle of the poster was a huge Tyrannosaurus Rex. He was standing in the middle of a ring of redwoods, lifting his head in what looked like an ear-splitting roar. In front of him, walking paths wove in and out of the trees. Beautiful flowers and plants were scattered in the shade. At the top of the poster, huge letters read: ASPEN HEIGHTS CONSERVATION PARK: EXPERIENCE NATURE, PAST AND PRESENT!

"This looks great!" said Kate. "You're really creative, Alexis."

"Thanks, but I couldn't have done it without your help! I'm not good at all of these computer programs." They printed off one copy of the poster and held it up.

"If we put these around town they should draw more people to the park!" said Alexis.

"Between those and the donations box, something *has* to happen," said Kate.

Mr. Howell brought home pizza, so the girls sat down with pepperoni and pineapple to watch the evening news. Alexis's mom had agreed they could watch TV from the table as long as Thad Swotter was reporting on Aspen Heights.

"It's on, Mom!" cried Alexis. "Come here!"

Nikki, the Channel 13 anchor, was talking to the camera. The picture in the upper right-hand corner of the television screen showed the giant head of Miss

Maria's Tyrannosaurus Rex.

"And here's Thad Swotter with the report," she said.

"Thanks, Nikki. Today was a scary day out here at Aspen Heights."

Alexis thought she recognized the scenery behind him. Soon the shape of the Tyrannosaurus loomed just behind the reporter, and she knew she was right.

"He's in the park!" Alexis said. "How did he get in after we closed?"

"Shh! Listen!" said Kate. Thad Swotter's voice barely cut through Alexis's swirling thoughts.

"Any doubts about strange happenings in this park were dissolved today when one of the mechanical dinosaurs actually *attacked* a young girl. As seen in this footage from a cell phone, the girl barely escaped with her life."

Thad Swotter's face was replaced by a video of Alexis diving for the ground as the Tyrannosaurus Rex's head fell toward her. Someone screamed, and at first Alexis thought it had come from the TV. It hadn't. It was her mother.

"Alexis Grace Howell!" she yelled. "What on earth is going on at that place? I said you could help at the park while Miss Maria is hurt, but *this*? It looks like things are getting dangerous."

Mrs. Howell stood with her hands on her hips, waiting for an explanation. Alexis's dad got up and walked toward the kitchen.

"More pizza, anyone?" he asked uneasily.

No one answered.

"It's not as bad as it looks, Mom," said Alexis. "You're always saying the news blows things out of proportion, remember? We were giving a tour, and. . .I'm not really sure what happened, but I'm fine!"

"Well, I don't like the idea of you being so close to those things. If they are prone to sudden movements, or if they break down—"

"We'll be more careful, Mom," said Alexis. "I promise! Please don't keep us away from the park. Miss Maria still needs us!"

"Fine, but I expect you two to be careful while you investigate. And from now on, I want daily updates. If I'm related to the detective, I shouldn't have to hear about everything on the news." Mrs. Howell called over her shoulder to the kitchen, "Now's a good time for that pizza, Rich!"

The next day, Alexis and Kate got to the park before anyone else did. They picked up all of the cameras, and as they walked through the park, they noticed that only one dinosaur had moved. As usual, it was one of the

Raptors. The girls put him back where he belonged and settled down in a back room of the visitors' center where they could use the computer.

Only three of the four cameras had taken pictures. Most of them were of nighttime creatures. The tail of a raccoon, or a flapping bat. There was a series of pictures of an owl picking up a mouse, no doubt planning to make a meal out of it.

"Wow! Those could be on the Discovery Channel!" said Alexis.

Thad Swotter and his cameraman made appearances in the pictures, too. Alexis got excited at first, thinking she'd catch them in action. But then she remembered the newscast. They weren't moving the dinosaurs. The camera had taken pictures of them while they were shooting their story. Alexis sighed.

"Is that all we have?" She was beginning to get frustrated. Usually when she was on a case she didn't have gadgets like Kate's cameras to help her. She thought for sure that they would make things easier. So far they hadn't.

Jerry entered the visitors' center and put two Cokes on the table.

"Thanks, Jerry!" said Alexis.

"No problem, Alex. Are those the pictures from last night?"

"Yeah," said Kate, "but we haven't seen anything so far."

Jerry opened his mouth to say something, but Alexis interrupted.

"Hey!" she said. "I want to know how that guy from Channel 13 got into the park after closing last night!"

"Easy," said Jerry. "I let him in."

"You *what*?" said Alexis.

"I. . .let. . .him. . .in." Jerry pushed Alexis's Coke toward her. "Drink up and don't worry! The news stories have been great for the park. It's like free advertising! Do you know how much it would cost to do a real TV commercial? It's a lot; I've checked. And the park was on the news for ten minutes last night!" He gave the can one last nudge. "Come on, Alex. It's Cherry Coke. . .your favorite."

Alexis took the can and shook her head. She couldn't believe that Jerry had let someone into the park after hours. Why was he suddenly friends with Thad Swotter anyway?

"Wait!" said Kate. "Look at this!"

There, in the corner of a picture, was a Raptor's nose.

"Remember the moved Raptor this morning?" said Kate. "I think we're going to find out how he got there, frame by frame!"

Both of the girls were on the edge of their seats. Kate

hit the button to look at the next picture.

Nothing.

But the third picture showed the Raptor's lizard head close-up. He was looking directly into the camera lens.

"It's like he knows it's there!" said Alexis. The following pictures reminded Alexis of a comic book: still pictures that told a story.

The Raptor's head again, looking away.

The Raptor's tail, like he was leaving.

The lens covered up by a bunch of leaves.

Leaves pulled away to reveal tons of Raptor footprints.

More dark leaves.

And finally, though the picture was a little fuzzy, a full-frame shot of the Raptor standing in the flowers on the other side of the path—just where they had found him this morning.

"Alexis?" said Kate.

"Yeah?"

"Are you thinking what I'm thinking?"

"That there wasn't even *one* picture of a human?" said Alexis.

"Exactly," Kate whispered. "Not even a finger. I don't understand, Alex."

"Me neither, Kate. I think the evidence is pointing to living, breathing dinosaurs."

"But that's impossible!" said Kate.

Alexis shrugged. Two days ago she would have laughed at the idea of dinosaurs coming to life in a Sacramento suburb.

Now she wasn't so sure.

Crucial Clue

Later that day, Kate sent copies of the digital pictures to the Camp Club Girls. Alex followed it with an e-mail.

TO: Camp Club Girls
SUBJECT: Notes
New Investigation: Could the dinosaurs really be alive?

Yes:

1. We have still not found any evidence of humans being involved. No prints and no people in the pictures from the hidden cameras.

2. The baby Triceratops moved without being plugged in—creepy.

3. The Tyrannosaurus Rex. . .enough said.

No:

1. As far as I know, electronic animals do not

*come to life. Otherwise, Disneyland would be in a
whole lot of trouble.*

*2. Also, I don't think the dinosaurs eat. None
of the plants near them are damaged. . .and Miss
Maria's cat hasn't gone missing yet.*

*Plan: Examine the footprints. Figure out if they
are real or if someone is faking them.*

The two Camp Club Girls waited until the park
was almost empty to make their move. They were
tired after another long day of giving tours, but at least
nothing crazy had happened today. Mrs. Smith had
been afraid that people would stay away because of the
Tyrannosaurus Rex, but no one seemed to care. In fact,
even more people had been on the trails today.

Alexis filled her pink Jansport with giant Ziploc bags
bulging with plaster of Paris. The white goop squelched
and squished as she and Kate headed through the park to
the most recent set of footprints.

One of the little green Raptors was separated from
the rest of the herd. It was the one that kept moving
around the park.

"I think he needs a name," said Kate.

"You're right," said Alexis. "How about Jogger?"

"It's perfect! Because he never stays in one place!"

Alexis opened a bag and poured a little of the plaster onto the ground. Then she grabbed Jogger and placed his feet gently in the white mush. After a minute or so, she lifted the dinosaur and wiped his feet. Then she put him back with his herd.

Kate was already comparing the prints in the plaster to the prints that were in the mud.

"They're a perfect match," she said. Alexis bent to examine them and found that Kate was right.

"Almost too perfect," Alexis said. Her thoughts were churning.

When a person walked, did they take the exact same step every time they moved? She thought about the many times she had sped up to catch someone, slowed down to wait, or tripped over something and stumbled.

No, she decided. *People's steps change all the time depending on where they are and how fast they're moving and what they're doing. If a girl is dialing a number on a cell phone, chances are her steps will slow down a bit and the footprints will be a bit deeper. . . .*

She walked around the Raptor area and noticed the same uniform prints everywhere. If these prints had been made by a living, breathing dinosaur, the creature had walked slowly and placed each step perfectly.

Alexis had never known any animal to move like that.

"Let's see what the bigger tracks tell us," she said.

At the site of the mother and baby Triceratops, the girls were disappointed. No fresh prints. Only those from the day Miss Maria got hurt. And emergency workers who helped Miss Maria into the ambulance had flattened all those prints.

While they searched, the girls got an unexpected visitor. Mrs. Smith trudged down the path carrying a heavy backpack.

"Hi, girls!" she said. "How's the investigation going?"

"Okay," said Alexis. "What are you doing?"

"I've got to switch out the battery for the baby Triceratops."

"The battery?" said Kate. "I thought all of the dinosaurs ran on generators."

"Well, most of them do," said Mrs. Smith. "Some of the smaller ones have battery packs. It makes them more versatile. You can put them in places that you couldn't fit a generator and they'll still move around. The batteries don't last long, though."

Mrs. Smith reached beneath the baby Triceratops and removed a large block. One side of it had greenish skin so it matched the dinosaur.

"I'll take this one back to the center and charge it.

Then I'll swap it again in a few days."

She dug the fresh battery out of her bag and snapped it into place. The baby dinosaur sprang to life. Its tail and head moved back and forth, and its eyes sparkled and blinked.

And it stuck out its tongue.

Alexis and Kate were stunned.

"It had a battery!" whispered Alexis.

"What's that?" said Mrs. Smith.

"Nothing," said Kate. The girls didn't want to admit that they had entertained thoughts about the baby dinosaur coming to life.

"Okay," said Mrs. Smith. "You girls take care! Miss Maria is supposed to come home today." Mrs. Smith took off back toward the visitors' center, leaving Kate smiling and Alexis writing furiously in her pink notebook.

"I can't believe it!" said Kate. "Its battery was just going dead! And it actually scared me!"

"Yeah," said Alexis. "You must have seen it using up the last little bit of power."

They were about to move on to the Tyrannosaurus tracks. Then Kate saw something in the mud that made her stop. She bent down and lifted a branch to reveal a track from the baby Triceratops.

"It's damaged!" said Kate. The back of the track was squashed.

"Perfect," she said dully. "The evidence has been contaminated by a squirrel or something."

"Wait!" Alexis bent down and examined the print.

"Kate," she said. "Can you go back and count how many toes the baby Triceratops has?"

"Sure," said Kate. In seconds she was kneeling near the dinosaur, dodging its moving horns. "Four!" she hollered back over her shoulder.

"I knew it!" said Alexis. "This print only has three toes! It's a fake, Kate!"

"Wow!" said Kate. "Whoever did this didn't do their homework, did they?"

"They didn't think anyone would look this close. But they don't know us, do they?" A triumphant smile stretched across Alexis's face. "Let's check out the Tyrannosaurus Rex."

There was no way Alexis and Kate could lift the Tyrannosaurus Rex leg, so they couldn't make a footprint in the plaster as they had with Jogger. They could only look as closely as possible to see if the foot seemed to match the tracks around it.

"Well," said Kate, "they sure look the same to me. The bottom of the tracks have some weird stripes on them, but I can't tell what they are."

"They do look the same," said Alexis. She handed

Kate a bag of plaster to pour into one of the prints. If they could take the print home, they could examine it more closely. Maybe they would see something they weren't noticing at the moment. Alexis walked around the dinosaur's huge legs again. She tried not to think about the head falling toward her.

"Kate?" Alexis asked. "How deep are those footprints?"

"How deep are they? About an inch. Why?"

"Don't you think an animal that weighed this much would make a deeper print in the mud?"

"Come to think of it, yes, probably," said Kate. "At home I have special equipment that could tell us the weight of a print this size and depth. Should I have my parents send it?"

"I don't think we need it," Alex said. "I think we can safely say something that weighs over a ton would have deeper prints."

Alexis followed the tracks away from the Tyrannosaurus Rex and into the forest.

"Everything looks normal—except, of course, dinosaur footprints in the dirt between the plants," Alexis called to Kate.

"*Between* the plants?" Kate asked.

Alexis gasped. "Wouldn't a dinosaur—especially a Tyrannosaurus Rex—do a lot of damage as he walked through a forest?"

"That's what I'm thinking," Kate said.

"I remember seeing a movie with a Tyrannosaurus Rex chasing something. Trees were flying everywhere, torn up by the roots. And whole bushes were stomped down," Alexis said. "I know it was just a movie, but. . ."

"Yeah, not even one of Miss Maria's tiniest flowers is bruised," Kate said. "How could a thirty-foot dinosaur navigate his way through a forest of tightly packed aspens? Especially without damaging one?"

"And look how close the prints are together," Kate added.

Alexis surveyed the prints and then looked back to the Tyrannosaurus Rex. "His legs are at least ten feet apart just standing there," she noted.

"And these are only four or five feet apart at the most," Kate said. "Unless the Tyrannosaurus Rex had tip-toed to the fence, these prints are fake!"

"And whoever made them cares enough about the plants not to damage them," Alexis pointed out.

"Look at this, Alex." Kate was kneeling down in the dirt, about three feet from the footprints. "When was the last time it rained?"

"A couple days ago," said Alexis. "Right before you got here."

"Okay," said Kate. "So how can there be mud for the

footprints? Look—the ground where the footprints are was apparently wet to make the tracks. But the path is dusty only a few feet away."

"You're right!" said Alexis. Someone was *making mud* so they could make the tracks.

Alexis got out her notebook to record all of her thoughts. The evidence was beginning to add up.

Evidence for fake tracks:

1. The Raptor tracks are too perfect—like someone picked up Jogger and sat him in the mud over and over, like a kid playing with a doll.

2. The Triceratops tracks are missing a toe.

3. The Tyrannosaurus Rex tracks are too close together, and did not damage plants.

4. There is no mud except where there are tracks.

Now Alexis was sure that someone must be planting the tracks. But who? And why would they do it? She and Kate still hadn't found any clues to help them answer that question.

"The plaster is almost dry," said Kate. "After we make the footprint, let's go see if Miss Maria's home."

"Good idea," said Alexis.

●—●—●

Alexis and Kate didn't make it to Miss Maria's house until after the park had closed for the day. They saw Miss

Maria sitting in her favorite chair on her front porch. She hugged an afghan tight around her shoulders, despite the summer heat. Her head was covered with a bright scarf.

As the girls climbed the porch steps, Alexis thought of how small she looked.

"Hello, girls! Come keep me company!"

Jerry came out of the front door. He was about to sit down, but Miss Maria stopped him.

"Jerry dear," she said, "could you get me a glass of lemonade, please?"

"Oh, sure!" said Jerry, and he disappeared back into the house.

Miss Maria beckoned Alexis and Kate with a crooked finger.

"Hurry!" she said in a whisper. "He won't be gone long!" She smiled like a little girl who thought she was keeping an important secret. "How is the investigation going?"

"Good and bad," said Alexis, looking over her shoulder at the screen door. She wondered why Miss Maria didn't want to talk about the investigation in front of Jerry. "We've just found out that the footprints are fake, so we're pretty sure the dinosaurs aren't coming to life."

Alexis thought Miss Maria might say something like, "Well, of course they're not coming to life!" But she didn't. She simply nodded and waited for Alexis to continue.

"The bad part is that we still don't have any evidence linking the incidents to any particular *person*."

"We think Thad Swotter could be doing it just to get a story," said Kate. "But that's just an idea. There's no evidence!"

Their frustration did not go unnoticed. Miss Maria smiled and leaned forward slightly.

"Of course there's evidence!" she said. "You just haven't found it yet! You think you've looked everywhere, but if that were the case you would have found something."

Noise from inside told them that Jerry was approaching. Miss Maria lowered her voice even more.

"Stop looking where you *expect* to find something. Instead, look where nothing should be."

Miss Maria nodded, as if she had just said the most obvious thing in the world. Alexis was confused, but before she could ask Maria to clarify, Jerry returned.

The girls accepted glasses of tart lemonade and stayed long enough to drink them before going back to the park. They returned to the Tyrannosaurus Rex to retrieve the dried footprint and to make sure they hadn't missed anything.

"I wish we could find something around here *besides* a dinosaur track!" said Kate. She picked up the bag of wet plaster they hadn't used and glared at it as if it were the reason they hadn't found what they needed.

"It will happen," said Alexis. "We just have to look where we wouldn't expect to find anything, like Miss Maria said."

Alexis wasn't sure this would work, but she had to try. She didn't know what else to do. So where was the last place they would expect to find a clue? Alexis pulled her brown curls into a tight ponytail and began to look.

At that moment, they heard a loud bark. They turned to see Biscuit flying down the trail toward them, his tongue and leash wagging in the wind.

"Where did he come from?" yelled Kate.

"Mom must have brought him!" said Alexis.

"Biscuit! *No!*"

But it was too late. The dog couldn't stop in time. He ran right into the Kate, knocking the bag of plaster from her arms and dumping it all over. The gooey white stuff splattered Kate and doused Alexis's foot before flowing beneath a nearby bush.

"Oh no!" said Kate. "I'm sorry, Alexis!"

"Don't worry about it," said Alexis. "After the plaster dries we can pick it right up." She knelt down to see how far under the bush the mess went, and she froze.

"Biscuit! You're a genius!" Alexis yelled. The dog jumped and wagged his tail, as if he had meant to help her all along.

"What is it, Alex?" asked Kate.

"Look for yourself!" Alexis lifted the lower branches of the bush so Kate could see. The plaster was barely trickling now. It ran over a few sticks before resting in a footprint.

Not a dinosaur print, but the obvious criss-cross pattern of a Converse All-Star.

Converse Connection

The next morning Mrs. Howell took the girls to a copy shop. Alexis wanted to print off a bunch of the posters they had made for the park. She would have done it at home, but her printer was out of colored ink. The twins had decided to print fifty copies of their latest creation: a full-color map of the neighborhood.

Mrs. Howell had been aggravated, but Alexis had to admit that the map was pretty good. The boys had marked all of the great hideouts, including a lump of honeysuckle and ivy near one corner that Alexis thought no one knew about. She was impressed. Maybe her little brothers had some detective skills hidden beneath their annoying natures.

Since their copier was out, Alexis decided on a more professional sign than she could do on her computer. She'd have the copy center make the signs full poster-sized and laminated so they'd last for a while.

Alexis dug her savings out of her pocket and put it on the copy counter.

"Honey," said her mother, "you don't have to spend all of that."

"I know," Alexis said. She had thought a lot about it, and she knew that this was what she wanted to do. Miss Maria had spent thousands of dollars trying to save her park. Alexis figured she could spend a few weeks of allowance. She could earn it back before Christmas, anyway, and if it would help the park, it was worth it.

"That will get you twenty full-color, laminated posters," said the freckled teenager behind the counter.

"Okay," said Alexis. "That's what we want, then!"

Half an hour later, Alexis and Kate walked out of the shop with the fresh posters draped over their arms. They were still warm from the printer. Mrs. Howell handed Alexis a paper bag full of tape and thumb tacks.

"Stick to the main road," she said. "I'm going to run something to the courthouse and I'll meet you at the coffee shop on the corner in an hour, okay?" She hugged Alexis and climbed into the red van, pointing it toward the white and silver dome of the capitol in the distance.

"So where do we start?" said Kate. The street was full of small hangouts. Internet cafés and coffee shops were everywhere.

They walked up and down the street leaving posters on community boards inside the shops. They even stuck a few to light posts and bus stops. The twenty posters were gone quickly, and Alexis wished she had saved more of her allowance.

"I guess that will have to do," she said to Kate. They were outside the corner coffee shop drinking iced lemonade the store manager had given them. She was a nice woman who hung one of their posters on the front of her pastry case. From their seat outside, the girls heard her tell each customer to visit the park and support Miss Maria.

Alexis was watching for her mother when something else caught her eye. A familiar-looking man entered the hardware store directly across the street.

"Kate! That's Thad Swotter's cameraman!" Alexis ran to the light post and slammed her hand against the button to activate the crosswalk. "Come on!" she said.

"Why are we following a cameraman?" asked Kate. The walk sign flashed green and the girls crossed the street.

"Maybe we'll hear something that will link Swotter to the dinosaurs," said Alexis.

"Do people usually let secrets slip to their neighborhood hardware store workers?" Kate asked with a laugh.

Alexis laughed, too.

"Probably not, but we have twenty minutes before

Mom picks us up, and sleuthing is more interesting than sitting on a corner."

The girls approached the hardware store windows but couldn't see through them. The windows were crowded with signs, shovels, and old newspaper articles with important headlines. Alexis poked her head around the open door. She couldn't see the cameraman.

She motioned to Kate and the two of them quietly walked inside. From behind a display of leather work gloves, they could see the cameraman. He was at the counter talking to the shop owner.

"If we get closer we may be able to hear what they're saying," Alexis said.

The girls inched their way around the outside aisle and stood behind a huge stack of red plastic buckets. Alexis glanced at the wall and pretended to be interested in the power tools hanging there.

"Need to replace my fence cutters," said the cameraman. "I'm helping a neighbor build a dog kennel, and I can't find mine."

"What size?" asked the hardware man.

"Pretty small. I only use them for chain-link fencing."

Alexis grabbed Kate's arm, causing her to jump. She tripped backward and fell against the tower of buckets.

Bam! The buckets flew around the girls.

Both the camera operator and the store owner turned toward the commotion. Alex and Kate scrambled to pick up all the buckets.

"Can I help you, ladies?" asked the hardware man.

"Uh, no thank you, sir," stuttered Alexis. Kate was chasing down a bucket that had rolled down the next aisle. "We were just looking at these, uh, tools."

The camera operator chuckled and the storeowner raised his eyebrows. Alexis turned and looked at the wall. She and Kate were standing in front of the biggest saw she had ever seen. Its round blade must have been three feet wide.

"Now why on earth would you need one of those?" asked the shop owner.

Alexis thought. She didn't want to lie, but she and Kate needed to get out of there in a hurry.

"You're right," she said with a nervous smile. "I probably don't need one this big. We'd better go down the road to the small saw store."

It was Kate's turn to grab Alexis by the arm. She dragged her out onto the sidewalk. The men's laughter echoed onto the busy street.

"Small saw store?" said Kate. "Good one."

"I'm sorry!" said Alexis. "I couldn't think of anything else!"

The girls hit the crosswalk button again and walked back across the street.

"Why did you freak out and grab my arm anyway?" asked Kate. "I wouldn't have knocked over those buckets if you hadn't scared me like that!"

They sat down at a small table outside the coffee shop again. The metal chairs were hot and burned their legs at first.

"The cameraman said he needed to replace his fence cutters," said Alexis. "He can't find his, and he said he only uses them on chain-link fencing!"

"Why did that make you grab me?" asked Kate.

"Remember? When I investigated the Tyrannosaurus Rex tracks, I followed them all the way to the fence. It had a huge hole. And it was a chain-link fence."

"Okay, so whoever is moving the dinosaurs cut a hole in the fence. Maybe that's how the person got into the park in the first place."

"I think they wanted people to think the Tyrannosaurus Rex did it," said Alexis. "To scare people, you know? What if the camera guy was helping Thad Swotter, and he lost his fence cutters that way? Or what if Swotter stole his fence cutters so he could cut the hole in the fence?"

"Maybe," said Kate. "It is a funny coincidence, but we

don't have any evidence."

She was right. Maybe they could go back to the fence this afternoon and look for the fence cutters. If they found them, they could connect Swotter—or at least his camera operator—to the mystery.

●—●—●

By the time the girls got to the park, the tours had already started. Since Jerry and Megan were leading people through the park, the area around the visitors' center was vacant—except for Jogger. He was looking at the entrance sign.

"Not again!" said Alexis.

Her emotions were torn. On one hand, she had a new crime scene to investigate. That was always exciting. On the other hand, she was angry at whoever was doing this to Miss Maria's park. She wondered if all detectives had the same struggle. The hunt was thrilling, but wasn't it sad that people were bad enough to make you hunt them in the first place?

"Kate, look!" Alexis had picked up Jogger to take him back to his fellow Raptors. There wasn't any mud, but in the loose dust was another human footprint. It was hardly visible. Kate whipped out her camera and snapped a few pictures.

"It's a Converse, like the other one," said Kate. She

bent to get a closer look. "Our suspect is getting sloppy."

"I know," said Alexis. "He didn't leave us a clue for days, and now we find two footprints in a row."

Just then, the girls heard a shout from the visitors' center. Two voices escalated. Someone wasn't happy.

"I think that's Mrs. Smith," said Alexis.

"Yeah. Let's see who else," said Kate. Alexis pushed on the front door and it swung wide, creaking slightly. The two arguing adults never even noticed.

Mrs. Smith's cheeks were bright red. Strands of dark hair swirled around her face. On the other side of the front desk, with his back to Alexis and Kate, was none other than Thad Swotter.

Only today he didn't have his little notebook and crazy tie. Instead, he wore faded jeans and a fitted polo. An Oakland Athletics ball cap hid his wild blond hair.

"Come on, Mrs. Smith!" Swotter said, trying not to yell. "You can't be serious!"

"I'm jut as serious as I was the last time, Thad," said Mrs. Smith. "I said no."

Swotter took off his hat and ran a hand through his gel-matted mop.

"At least think about it," he pleaded.

"Thad, no. I'm not interested." Mrs. Smith wasn't yelling anymore. She just looked tired. "You're welcome to look around the park, Thad, or shoot another crazy story, but this conversation is over." Mrs. Smith gestured toward the two girls. Swotter noticed them for the first time.

"Fine," he said, jamming his hat back on. "I'll go. Enjoy your day here at Bible Land!"

"What's that supposed to mean?" fired Mrs. Smith. Her anger was back.

"I'm talking about the Old Bat's crazy greenhouse! It's not like you guys are giving tours through Jerusalem! A visitor can't bend to smell a rose without getting a cross stabbed in his eye!"

"Come on, Thad," said Mrs. Smith. "I know you're angry, but you're exaggerating just a little—"

"Am I?" Thad Swotter was far from composed. His face was a mixture of red and white blotches, and sweat was running down his neck.

"I've told you before that you should get rid of all that stuff!" he said. "People don't want to see Jesus Thorns, or the Lily of the Valley. They come here to see the redwoods and California plants—and they *don't* want to hear that any *God* planted them! People would be lining up to give this place money if it weren't for that stuff!"

He turned and stomped past Alexis and Kate, slamming the door behind him. The girls cautiously approached the desk.

"Was he asking for another interview?" asked Alexis.

"Yeah, something like that," said Mrs. Smith with a weak smile. She pushed a small bouquet of flowers off the desk and into the trash can.

"Those were pretty!" said Kate.

"They smelled funny," said Mrs. Smith. "What are you girls up to today?"

"Just looking for a break," said Alexis.

"Well, you're welcome to grab a Coke out of the fridge and sit in here for a while," said Mrs. Smith.

"Not that kind of break, Mrs. Smith," said Alexis. She grabbed two sodas anyway and handed one to Kate. "I meant we need a lucky break in this case. We found some good clues yesterday. We're going to see where they lead us."

Alexis told Mrs. Smith all about the footprints being fake and the posters they hung up.

"Those posters should help," said Mrs. Smith. "Thanks for doing that. Maybe when the donation box fills up a little more we should use the money to print more of them. Then we can hang some in other areas of town."

Alexis could see Mrs. Smith's bad mood evaporating. This was good, because Alexis had a favor to ask. She knew from an experience with her grandma that angry adults were not much help when it came to investigating. It was really hard to get good information out of someone who had just turned her hair purple on accident.

"Mrs. Smith, can I ask you something?" Alexis said.

Mrs. Smith was sipping her Diet Coke, but she nodded.

"We were thinking about camping out in the park," Alexis said. "You know, like a stakeout? Do you think that would be okay?"

"That should be okay," said Mrs. Smith. "But we should double-check with Maria first. I'll talk to her this afternoon."

Kate and Alexis left the visitors' center. They were going to inspect the new footprint some more and compare it to the one they had found the day before. Alexis was in the lead, and as she turned the corner she ran right into Thad Swotter.

Bam! The force of the impact threw her backward. She landed hard on her backside a few feet away. Swotter juggled his cell phone, trying not to drop it. He grumbled an "excuse me" and began walking quickly toward the parking lot, still talking on the phone.

"Oh my goodness!" exclaimed Alexis.

"I know," said Kate. "He didn't even offer to help you up! Are you okay?"

"No! Not that!" said Alexis. She rolled onto her knees and pointed after the reporter. "Look at his shoes!"

There went Thad Swotter—newly famous Sacramento reporter—tromping to his car in a very muddy pair of Converse All-Stars.

CHAPTER 7

Dinosaurs in the Dark

"I still can't believe you guys are doing this!" said Jerry. He was bent over, trying to put Alexis's tent together. He obviously had no idea what he was doing.

"That's the door, Jerry!" said Alexis, stooping to help. "You can't put it against the ground! How will we get in?"

Alexis shook out the tent and laid it right-side up. She grabbed a handful of slender plastic rods and went to work. In minutes, she had the tent standing.

"Here," Alexis teased, passing Jerry a hammer. "You can handle putting the stakes in the ground, right? Just stick them through those loops at the corners and pound them in."

Alexis and Kate had chosen the clearing near the Raptors for their overnight stakeout. They would set up a night-vision digital camcorder and be ready to catch Thad Swotter in the act if he struck again tonight. Even if he showed up and left after seeing the girls' tent, maybe the camera would get a good shot of him first.

"So why *are* you doing this?" asked Megan. She was helping Kate set up the video camera on a hidden stump.

"I told you, Meg," said Alexis. "Nothing else is working. We need to get to the bottom of this before someone gets hurt."

"What makes you so sure someone is going to get hurt?" asked Jerry. "Nothing bad has happened so far. The park is packed every day!"

"Um, Miss Maria was hurt," said Kate. Her voice was almost a whisper—her head hanging down as if she was speaking to her shoes. "She wouldn't have been climbing on the Triceratops if it weren't for those footprints, remember? And what about the day the Tyrannosaurus Rex's head nearly fell on Alex? That could have been because someone was messing around it while making the footprints."

Jerry didn't answer, but he raised his eyebrows. Alexis knew what he was thinking: Miss Maria shouldn't have climbed on top of the dinosaur without anyone around to help. But Alexis also knew that whether Miss Maria was right or wrong, it all came down to the footprints. They had started this whole mess.

"Look at the big picture, guys," said Alexis. "Even if no one ever gets hurt, damage has been done to the park. A whole section of the fence has to be replaced because there's a huge hole in it."

"And besides," Kate added, "whoever's messing around with the dinosaurs might hurt them. I was looking at animated dinosaurs on a Web site that sells special effects. Some of these dinosaurs cost up to twenty thousand dollars to replace!"

"If something happened to one, Miss Maria might have to use all her savings to pay for it and have to close the park."

Jerry didn't say anything else. He went to Alexis's backpack, pulled out some chips, and chomped moodily while the girls finished setting up camp.

Alexis was aggravated. She loved investigating, but she knew this was taking up valuable time. The sooner she found out who was doing this, the sooner she could focus on Miss Maria's real problem—bringing in visitors and money even after the dinosaurs were gone. All of this craziness was keeping them from finding a solution to the real problem.

Alexis tried to get Jerry and Megan to stay with them, but they were too freaked out about sleeping in the park. Jerry didn't camp. Alexis had learned that much by watching him try to put the tent together. Megan just kept making excuses.

"What if the Tyrannosaurus Rex steps on me in my

sleep?" she joked as the group headed in to dinner. Their camp was not far from Jerry and Megan's house, which was just on the edge of the park near the visitors' center. Mrs. Smith had invited the girls to eat dinner there before they began their campout.

Dinner was great, except for Jerry's jokes. He kept telling Alexis and Kate to watch out for dinosaur manure, or to keep their snacks locked up so they wouldn't attract the bears. . .or the Tyrannosaurus Rex.

"I heard they found a new species of squirrel in the Sierras," Jerry said with a mouth full of enchilada.

"Really?" said Kate, drawn in by her love of animals.

"Yeah, vampire squirrels. Watch your necks!"

Alexis shivered. For some reason, she couldn't swallow the bite she had just taken.

"Jerry, stop it!" said Mrs. Smith.

Alexis would normally have laughed all night at Jerry's jokes, but she was about to sleep in a dark forest. For that reason, none of the jokes seemed very funny. It wasn't like Jerry to be mean. Maybe he didn't realize he was scaring them.

Kate spoke up as the two of them returned to camp. "If I didn't know better, I would say he didn't want us out here."

"I don't know," said Alexis. "He's probably just trying

to scare us because he's embarrassed. Think about it! He was too chicken to stay out here, and two *girls* are going to show him up. Either that or he's just being a boy. By definition they're obnoxious!"

Biscuit tromped along beside Kate on his leash. His presence calmed their nerves, and by the time they reached the Raptor clearing, their laughter echoed through the trees.

The two Camp Club Girls snuggled down into their sleeping bags. They pulled out Kate's computer and filled in the Camp Club Girls until the battery died. Then they fell asleep.

●—●—●

It was still pitch black outside when Kate woke up to find Biscuit's wet nose in her face. He nudged her and then walked over Alexis to the door of the tent.

"What is it?" asked Alexis. She sat up and rubbed her sleepy eyes.

"It's just Biscuit," said Kate. "I think he has to go to the bathroom."

Kate unzipped the tent and led her whining puppy outside. After a second, her head popped back in the tent.

"Forgot the flashlight!" she said. She grabbed Alexis's lantern and went to supervise the excited puppy. Alexis was just about to drift back to sleep when she heard Kate call in a frantic whisper.

"Alexis! Get out here!"

"What is it?" asked Alexis. She fought her way out of her sleeping bag and shoved on her shoes. Biscuit was pulling frantically on his leash, choking himself in his excitement to explore. Kate was standing in the middle of the camp, shining her light on the ground.

"Look!" she said.

"No way!" said Alexis. The camp was absolutely crowded with Raptor footprints. When the girls had gone to bed, the little green dinosaurs had been in their place on the other side of the clearing. Kate shined the light around the edge of camp. Little pairs of eyes glinted in the beam.

They were surrounded.

Alexis didn't know what was creepier, being stared at by a ring of dinosaurs or the thought that someone had been here to move them *while the girls were sleeping.*

"My camera's gone!" cried Kate. Sure enough, the camera she and Megan had hidden on the stump was gone. Jogger was sitting in his place. In the dancing moonlight, he looked as if he was laughing.

"Great!" said Alexis. "We slept through everything!"

Alexis had never been angrier. She thought for sure

this campout would lead them to the identity of the dinosaur mover. Instead, they were standing in the dark, looking at a bunch of new footprints that had been put there right under their noses. And now Kate's newest video camera was gone. Alexis reminded herself to add theft to the list of crimes in her notebook.

"Someone is making fun of us!" Alexis huffed. "Every time we get a little closer to figuring things out, we get stumped!"

"I know," said Kate. "It's *extremely* frust–"

Slam!

A loud noise ricocheted through the forest. The girls stood still as statues. Biscuit's ears were standing up, listening for any sign of movement.

"That sounded like a car door," whispered Alexis. She looked at her watch. "Who would be out here at two thirty in the morning?"

"Someone up to no good!" said Kate.

"Come on!" said Alexis. "Maybe it's Thad. Let's sneak up on him. We can't let him see us, but maybe we'll be able to see *him*."

Kate nodded and the girls started picking their way through the forest. They kept off the paths. The last thing they wanted was to run right into a criminal.

Alexis breathed deeply. Her heart slammed against

her rib cage in a frantic rhythm, and she was sure it could be heard a mile away. The girls picked a path through the aspens and dodged the Tyrannosaurus. In the moonlight, the giant reptile looked more than alive. They crossed the Triceratops meadow, and Alexis took in a sharp breath.

The baby Triceratops was missing.

"Look," whispered Kate. "Footprints." Alexis noticed they had only three toes.

The girls followed the fake Triceratops footprints through the meadow. They stopped abruptly at a clump of large bushes. The girls veered to the left to walk around when they heard a loud *click*. A flash of light temporarily blinded them.

Alexis ducked down behind the bush. She pulled Kate down beside her and waited for her eyes to adjust. Spots danced in front of her face like stars.

They heard footsteps. The rustle of dry pine needles. *Click. Flash!*

Alexis edged toward the sound. She peeked around the bush and had to cover her mouth to keep from crying out.

Thad Swotter was standing on the other side of their hiding place. His green and yellow A's hat was on backwards, and he was snapping pictures of the newly moved baby Triceratops.

Kate signaled Alexis to keep quiet and crawled

deeper into the bush. She positioned her spy watch to point toward Swotter. The small watch, Alexis knew, was able to take pictures. The next time Swotter took a picture, Kate did, too, so he didn't notice the flash of her watch.

After a few more minutes, the reporter turned and walked back through the trees.

"Come on!" whispered Alexis. The girls took off after him, keeping back so they wouldn't be seen.

They were heading northeast through the park, toward the highway. Thad Swotter went faster, and the girls struggled to keep up. Alexis caught her foot on a tree root and stumbled.

"Whoa!" she said. She regained her balance, glad that she hadn't fallen, but Kate grabbed her and pulled her behind a tree.

Swotter had stopped and was shining a flashlight in their direction. The light panned back and forth, igniting the forest around them and casting thick shadows.

"Who's there?" Swotter called. He sounded nervous. Alexis wanted to make some dinosaur noises, just to scare him, but she kept quiet.

"Stupid forest," Swotter said to himself. He turned away again. Alexis noticed that the steps were quicker and his breathing labored. He was running.

The girls followed the spooked reporter to the edge of the park. He climbed over the fence and jogged to the Channel 13 news van parked on the shoulder of Highway 80. Kate was about to take another picture, but a big, masculine hand reached over her shoulder and grabbed her arm.

"I wouldn't do that if I were you."

From Theater to Threat

"Really, I wouldn't do that," said Jerry. "He'll see your flash."

Alexis and Kate spun around.

"Jerry, you scared us to death!" whispered Alexis. "What are you doing here anyway?"

"Couldn't sleep, so I thought I'd check on you," he said. "You weren't in camp, so I got worried."

"We're *fine!*" said Alexis. Swotter's van was gone. She turned and tromped through the forest toward their tent. She didn't care how loud she was anymore, now that the danger of being seen had passed.

The girls couldn't bring themselves to climb back into their sleeping bags and sleep after their discovery. So they sat up in their tent instead, telling Jerry all about it until the sun came up. Then they packed up camp and walked to Jerry's house for breakfast.

Alexis was sure she had solved the mystery. First, there were Thad Swotter's muddy Converse shoes, which matched the only human footprint they had found so far.

Now they had caught him in the park in the middle of the night. He *hadn't* been filming a story for the news. Why would he sneak around the park so late at night if he wasn't moving the dinosaurs?

She and Kate had every detective's dream: undeniable evidence. They hadn't just seen Swotter at the scene of the crime. They had a *picture* of him there! There was no way he could deny it—Alexis just had to figure out how to confront him.

Mrs. Howell picked the girls up around ten and took them home. They went up to Alexis's room and finally fell asleep. Alexis slept until lunchtime, when the twins ran in screaming.

"Lexi! Get up! Get up! Get up!"

They leapt onto the bed, pinning Alexis beneath four bony knees.

"Get up! It's family movie day, remember? Come on!"

And just like that they were gone, pounding down the stairs leaving Alexis and Kate to wipe the sleep from their eyes.

"Family movie day?" asked Kate through a cavernous yawn.

"Yeah," said Alexis. "Once a month my parents take a day off and we all go see a movie together. It's tradition!" She ran into the bathroom, ran a brush through her hair, and burst back into her room to change her T-shirt. "Today it's the new Glenda McGee movie!"

"Yes!" Kate exclaimed. She rushed to take Biscuit outside before they left.

Alexis and Kate were just as excited as the twins. They had been waiting six months for *Glenda McGee: Hacking Hero* to come out in theaters. Glenda McGee was a teen computer genius who solved mysteries. Kate enjoyed all of the gadgets she used, even though most of them were fictional. The twins liked the fight scenes, where Glenda's cheerleading jumps became killer roundhouse kicks. Alexis just loved the way the heroine balanced saving the world with getting her nails done and studying for exams.

The movie was amazing, and not just because the Howells bought popcorn, drinks, and a ton of candy. The girls talked about the twists and turns of the plot as they walked to the car.

"I can't believe that ending!" said Alexis.

"I know!" said Kate. "The butler was the bad guy! But he was so nice!"

"Yeah! He actually *helped* Glenda solve pieces of the mystery. It was just enough to keep her thinking he was good."

The family piled into the car and Alexis's mind

105

strayed back to the case the Camp Club Girls were still trying to solve. The movie had gotten her excited. She may not be able to do a double-back flip over a burning car to save the world, but she *could* take down Thad Swotter and save Miss Maria's park.

"Mom," she said, "would it be too far out of the way to take us back to Aspen Heights?"

"No, that's fine," said Mrs. Howell. "I have to run a few errands anyway, and it will be easier if six of us aren't running around the grocery store. I'll drop you girls off and then pick you up on my way home."

Alexis had printed the picture of Thad Swotter with the baby Triceratops before she had left the house that morning. She pulled it out of her pink notebook and examined it as they drove. This picture truly looked suspicious. Should they show it to Maria or Mrs. Smith and let the adults handle things?

No. She was sure he was guilty, but what if he weaseled his way out of it? The other adults were sure to believe him over her. Alexis needed to be completely sure about Thad Swotter before she tattled on him.

What would Swotter say when she and Kate showed him the picture?

●—●—●

The girls didn't see any signs of the news van when

they pulled onto the Aspen Heights parking lot. Disappointed, Alexis and Kate entered the visitors' center. Mrs. Smith, Jerry, and Megan were inside, taking a break from leading tours.

"Jerry tells me you girls have things figured out," said Mrs. Smith. She passed Alexis and Kate popsicles from the freezer.

"We think so," said Alexis, opening her banana treat. She wanted to tell Mrs. Smith what they had found but decided to wait. "What are you working on?"

Mrs. Smith had a huge pile of paper in front of her. She was reading through it, highlighting paragraphs and making notes on the edges.

"It's a proposal for the school board," said Mrs. Smith. "I've talked to a couple of local principals, and they might make Aspen Heights a regular field trip location."

"That sounds great," said Kate.

"Yeah. If this works out, it would prove that the park is valuable to the community. We may be able to get some funding."

"Then Miss Maria could keep the park open!" said Alexis. "Dinosaurs or no dinosaurs!"

"That's the plan," said Mrs. Smith. "Say a prayer. The school board meeting is in two days, and I have to get past them before I can advertise to all of the teachers."

"I'm sure it'll be fine!" said Alexis.

"Oh no," said Mrs. Smith.

"Of course it will be!" said Kate.

"No, it's not that," said Mrs. Smith. "Channel 13 just showed up. I'm going in the back room. . .and I'm *not* doing any interviews." She got up and closed the door to her office.

"Well, *we* want an interview, don't we, Kate?" Alexis threw away her sticky popsicle stick and ran outside. Thad Swotter was coming straight to the visitors' center, so Alexis and Kate just waited near the door. Alexis took out her pink notebook and flipped to the page where she had written down a list of questions for their suspect.

Swotter started to walk past them, but Alexis stepped in front of the door at the last second, and he almost ran into her.

"Whoa! Don't want to knock you over again!" he joked. "Excuse me, girls. I'm looking for Mrs. Smith. Is she in there?"

"Yes," said Alexis. "But she's busy."

"I'm not asking for an interview," he said. "I don't even have the camera today. Can you just tell her I'm here?"

"Actually, Mr. Swotter, we were hoping we could ask you a couple of questions."

Swotter raised his eyebrows.

"A little reporter in the making, huh?" he said, looking pleased. "Ask away."

"Where were you last night?"

"I gave the nightly six o'clock report, as usual," he said. "Which takes a lot of preparation and—"

"And after that?" asked Kate.

"I, uh. . .ate dinner and went home." Swotter shifted his weight and crossed his arms. Alexis's dad had told her that this was a defensive move—people stood like that when they felt threatened or uncomfortable. He saw people do it in court a lot. Alexis was glad she was making Swotter uncomfortable. It meant they were headed in the right direction.

Alexis scribbled answers in her notebook. She had a bunch of questions she could have asked, but why ask tons of questions when one direct shot would get the answers she needed? Besides, if he wasn't expecting it he might accidentally confess. She took a deep breath.

"And why were you wandering around Aspen Heights at two thirty this morning moving our dinosaurs?" she asked.

"Well, I—*what*? Now wait just one minute." Swotter was definitely caught off guard. He swept his hat off his head and crossed his arms again. "I never touched any of your dinosaurs."

"But you admit you were here?" asked Alexis casually. Swotter's eyes narrowed. He flattened out his mouth, as if to keep it from talking. His nostrils flared. Alexis thought about her father. His nostrils never flared, but when his mouth went flat like that, she knew better than to push him. It meant he was getting angry. Alexis remembered Thad's argument with Mrs. Smith the other day and took a step backward. Would he start yelling and screaming at *them*?

"You *were* here, right?" said Kate softly.

Alexis took the picture out of her notebook and handed it to him.

"It was you!" Swotter said. "I knew there was someone out there! You scared me to death!" Alexis expected him to try to make excuses. She expected him to defend himself, or to confess, or get mad. But Swotter did something far less predictable. He laughed.

"Wow," he said. "You girls are sneaky." He ruffled his hair and crammed his hat back on.

"Sure, I was here last night," he continued. "I come every night, at about midnight, to see which dinosaurs have moved, then I take pictures of them. That's how I get my stories in time for the morning news. We're the only channel that has pictures that early! My boss loves me for it. I fell asleep on my couch last night—didn't make it out here until two."

Alexis put her hands on her hips and raised her eyebrows.

"I know what you're thinking," said Swotter. "It's no secret that I don't love this place. You think I'm moving the dinosaurs to scare people away? Or maybe just to get a good story?" The girls' silence told him he was right.

"Look around," he said. "This place is packed! If I wanted Aspen Heights to go under, I wouldn't do something that brings in *more* business."

"So you admit that you want the park to go under?" asked Alexis.

"No, I said *if*. Look, I may not agree with all of Miss Maria's beliefs, but there's no reason to take the park down because of it! Maybe you and your friends should take a closer look at things. I'm not the bad guy everyone around here seems to think I am."

Swotter moved toward the door of the visitors' center but seemed to think better of it. He sighed and walked wearily back to his news van.

"Come on. Let's take a walk so we can think," Kate said, walking through the door into the park.

Alexis was confused. "I was so sure we had figured it out!" she said.

"Me, too," said Kate.

"Who else could it have been, Kate? All of the evidence points to him!"

"You mean his shoes?" asked Kate. "Besides seeing Swotter taking pictures, that's the only real evidence we have. Look around! Those shoes are in style. Half the people in this park are wearing them."

Kate was right. Alexis counted five pairs of black Converse, two pairs of pink, and a group of teens wearing them in crazy plaids. She even saw a two-year-old toddling around in a pair. . .and this was just one section of the park.

"You're right, Kate," said Alexis. "And last night we didn't see him move any dinosaurs. We only saw him taking pictures, and he admitted to that."

How could she have been so blind? Looking back, Alexis could see that the evidence pointing toward Thad Swotter had always been a little shaky. She had made a huge mistake.

When she first met Swotter, he had been rude. She had *wanted* him to be guilty, so she had seen every piece of evidence through her prejudice. She had made a judgment based on emotions, not on evidence.

"I guess we need a new suspect," said Alexis.

"Nonsense!" said Kate. "I mean, we can keep investigating and following evidence, but we shouldn't drop Thad Swotter as a suspect too easily."

"But Kate, he said—"

"Alexis." Kate stopped walking. She stood in the middle of the trail facing Alexis. "Get a grip. Since when did the police stop investigating someone just because they *said* they didn't do it? Everyone *says* they're innocent."

"You're right," said Alexis. "We'll stick with the evidence this time, though. If it points to Swotter, we'll question him again. If not, then maybe it will point to someone else."

They passed the entrance sign just as Mrs. Howell pulled into the parking lot. Alexis was climbing in when Jerry ran out of the visitors' center.

"Hey, Alexis! Wait! Someone left this for you on the front desk." He handed a small white envelope though the car window.

"Who was it?" asked Alexis. Jerry shrugged.

"No one saw. It was just there on the desk."

"Then how did you know it was for—oh." Alexis saw her name on the outside of the envelope. Jerry smiled and waved as Mrs. Howell pulled away. The car was crowded, so Alexis didn't open the envelope just yet. What could it be?

Maybe it was an anonymous check. If the amount

was huge—big enough to save the park—then whoever left it might have felt better putting it on the desk instead of the donations box. But why would they give it to her, and not Mrs. Smith or Miss Maria?

The car pulled in the driveway and Alexis and Kate tore up the stairs. Finally, they were in her room, at a safe distance from the prying eyes of the twins.

Alexis opened the envelope. To her dismay, there was no check. It was just a folded piece of white paper. Maybe a note from Miss Maria, or Mr. Bell. . .

She noticed that her name on the envelope was not handwritten—it looked like the work of an old typewriter. Who would take the time to type on an envelope? Alexis dropped the envelope on her bed and unfolded the note. The words typed there stole her breath away.

STOP SNOOPING, OR ELSE. . .

Chapter 9

Litter and Lip Gloss

TO: Camp Club Girls
SUBJECT: New Stuff

1. Creepy note—who could it be from? Is someone just messing with us, or could it be a real threat?

2. Thad Swotter—says he isn't our guy. . .we're not so sure.

Updates:

1. Donations box total to date: $24.37 (obviously not enough to save the park. . .)

2. Posters—most of them covered up by other announcements. Mrs. Smith's school board idea might be our last chance.

"It's ready!" said Kate.

She was kneeling on Alexis's bed in front of the open laptop. On the screen was a live picture of Aspen Heights. Kate had spent most of the day rigging up a web camera in the park. She used Mrs. Smith's Internet connection at the visitors' center, so now they could watch the park all night from the safety of Alexis's room. "I'll send a link to the other Camp Club girls so they can take shifts and help us watch."

"Six sets of eyes are better than two," Alex agreed.

The girls wanted to watch the park by night again, and this was the best way to do it. Spending another night out in the forest was out of the question, since Mrs. Howell had found out about Thad Swotter wandering around after hours. They didn't admit it, but Alexis and Kate were freaked out, too. Not really because of Swotter, but because of the note. They definitely didn't want to be alone in the dark woods if someone was angry enough to hurt them.

Kate placed the web camera near the Raptor clearing. Since Jogger moved every night, they figured some action would probably occur there. It was also pretty close to the visitors' center. That made it easier for Kate to run the tiny wire all the way from the computer in the visitors' center to the tree with the camera in it.

"Everything's set," said Kate, falling back onto the pillows. "Now all we have to do is wait."

"Shouldn't be too long," said Alexis. "Swotter said he usually sneaks into the park to take pictures around midnight. That means whoever moves the dinosaurs and leaves the footprints—if it isn't him—must do it before midnight."

The digital clock on Alexis's bed stand flashed 9:40.

At first they just stared at the screen. Their eyes stung, and they were afraid to blink. After all, the dinosaurs had moved right under their noses the other night. Someone *had* tromped around leaving footprints only feet away from their pillows, and they hadn't heard a thing. Alexis was determined not to miss out *this* time.

Finally, after twenty minutes with no movement on the camera, they started playing games to pass the time.

The clock read 10:30.

They ate chips and managed to drink an entire two-liter bottle of Mountain Dew. They couldn't have fallen asleep if they wanted to, and Mrs. Howell had been in twice to ask them to be quiet.

It was 11:15.

They had tossed the deck of cards off the bed and were playing Clue for the third time when Kate got a text from Bailey, asking if she was watching the screen.

"It's happening!" Kate yelled. She clapped her hand over her mouth, hoping she hadn't awakened Alexis's family.

"I know it's happening!" said Alexis. "I'm about to beat you again! I think it was Colonel Mustard, with the wrench, in the conserva—"

"No, Alexis! Look at the computer!"

Alexis dropped her game piece. The bushes across the path from the camera were rustling. To the left of the screen, closer this time, something flashed—the white tip of a Converse shoe.

"If our Converse guy is near the camera, what just moved in the bushes?" asked Kate.

"There must be two of them," said Alexis.

They watched the screen for five minutes. Nothing moved. All of a sudden, the screen went dark. No more dinosaurs, no more bushes. Just blackness.

Or was it green?

Alexis lay down on the bed and got as close to the screen as she could. She pushed a button with a little sun on it and the picture got brighter. The blotch of black lightened, turning into a bunch of three-pointed shapes that were gleaming in the moonlight.

"They're leaves," said Alexis. "The camera has been blocked by a bunch of leaves."

"I thought Jerry and I rigged the camera far enough away from the plants," mused Kate.

Just then, the leaves moved. Jogger was missing, and his footprints were everywhere.

"No!" cried Alexis. "We missed it again!"

"AAAHH!" both girls screamed and fell off the bed. Game pieces and chips flew everywhere. Somewhere in the house a door banged. Angry footsteps stomped down the hall, but that's not what had frightened them. Something had suddenly jumped into the camera's line of sight. Alexis crept back to the foot of the bed and peeked over the footboard at the computer.

Jogger was looking directly into the camera. His head bent to the side, curious maybe—and then he was gone.

•—•—•

The next morning the sun glowed brilliantly, as if it didn't know—or didn't care—that Alexis's case was falling apart. The girls were running out of time. The truth was that the Camp Club Girls *still* didn't have much to go on. Last night's watch hadn't accomplished much.

The girls walked slowly through the park. Alexis wanted to examine the new crime scene, and they needed to get the web cam out of the tree.

"I still can't believe it!" said Alexis. "Jogger looked right into our camera!"

"Yeah," said Kate. "That means that the people moving him must have found it. They know we're watching them now."

"It's like they are making fun of us. I thought you said you hid the camera!" said Alexis.

119

"I did!" said Kate.

"Okay," said Alexis. "I'm sorry. Let's focus on what we *did* find out last night." She flipped to a clean page in her notebook and began to scribble.

"We know that there are probably *two* people involved," she said. "Maybe one to move the dinosaurs and one to place the prints? The first person is Converse Guy. He left his print at some other scenes, and we caught a glimpse of his shoe last night. The other person was hiding in the bushes. Man! If it weren't for those stupid leaves we might have seen their faces!"

When they reached the Raptor area they headed to the bush on the far side of the trail. Alexis hoped Criminal Number 2 had left some kind of clue. The search didn't take long, but it wasn't because Alexis was fast. There simply wasn't anything to find except an empty water bottle with a bright pink lip gloss around the rim.

"Maybe this means one of the suspects is a girl," said Alexis.

"Maybe," said Kate. "Or maybe some visitor was just too lazy to walk across the clearing to the trash can."

Kate walked over to look at the camera. A lump of oily leaves wilted on the ground beneath it. It looked like someone had pulled them up by the roots. Kate reached down to pick them up.

Alexis glanced over her shoulder. She dropped the water bottle she had been examining and yelled, "Kate, stop! That's poison oak!"

Kate's fingers stopped an inch from the plant. Alexis joined her and poked the leaves with a stick.

"It looks like someone yanked these out of the ground," she said.

"Don't they look like the leaves we saw covering the camera last night?" asked Kate. "I knew there weren't any leaves where I hung it. What if someone covered the lens on purpose?"

"You're right," said Alexis. "I bet they hid until the leaves were in place. Then one came out of the bushes to do the prints and the other one grabbed Jogger. After they were done, they moved the leaves and gave us a show!"

Alexis felt sure she was right. It made sense that the criminals wouldn't want to be seen on tape. But why cover the camera instead of simply unplugging it? And why dance Jogger in front of the lens?

Alexis could handle a lot without getting angry. The heat of a California summer was bearable. Long lines at her favorite amusement park were no problem. She could even deal with her little brothers when they hid all over the house, waiting to scare her as she walked by. But when her suspects started to tease her, her patience wore thin.

"These people are playing games with us, Kate. It's getting on my nerves." She kicked the poison oak back into the forest, away from the trail. Miss Maria didn't need park visitors going home with rashes.

Rashes.

Suddenly Alexis remembered Sydney telling her about poison oak when they were at camp. "If you get into it, it can give you a bad rash," Sydney explained. She had told Alexis about the rash she'd gotten while in the woods with her park ranger aunt.

Alexis couldn't believe she hadn't thought of it sooner. This was huge. If the Converse Guy touched the poison oak, he would have an awful rash by now. He could taunt her all he wanted—Alexis finally felt like she was ahead. She scribbled in her notebook:

Keep an eye out for someone with a rash. . .and someone wearing bright pink lip gloss.

Alexis picked up the plastic bottle and stuffed it into her backpack. She was excited to continue her investigation now that she had a break in the case, but they had to get the camera down first. They headed back through the park to a storage area behind the visitors' center, where they could get a ladder.

The girls approached the cleared area that held a small greenhouse, piles of terra cotta pots, and a small storage shed where Miss Maria kept her tools and equipment. A rope hanging between two trees sported a sign that read, EMPLOYEES AND VOLUNTEERS ONLY! Alexis stepped over the sign and almost fell on Jerry. He was covered up to his knees in manure.

Alexis and Kate almost collapsed in a fit of giggles.

"It's time to fertilize," said Jerry, leaning on his shovel. "There's no need to laugh so hard!"

"I'm sorry," wheezed Alexis. "It's just, I really needed a laugh!"

"Glad I could help. What brings you back here, anyway?"

"We need to get the web cam down," said Alexis. "I was coming to get a ladder out of the shed."

Jerry was out of the manure in seconds. He reached the shed before Alexis had taken two steps.

"You don't want to go in there! Really, it's unorganized and crazy—there's stuff everywhere. You might get hurt."

"You've been in there," said Alexis, pointing to the shovel. "And you're just fine."

Jerry crossed his arms and shook his head.

"Well, since you're being so chivalrous, can *you* get

us the ladder?" said Alexis. "We need to take care of that camera before something happens to it. We already lost one of Kate's cameras the night we camped out."

"Don't worry," said Jerry, glancing over his shoulder at the wooden door. It was cracked open an inch. He backed up and kicked it closed. "I'll get the camera down for you in a bit, when I'm done here."

"Okay," said Alexis. "Thanks." The girls walked away, perplexed. Why was Jerry acting so weird? Maybe he was embarrassed about how messy he had let the shed get while Miss Maria was away.

"Boy, it's hot out here," Kate exclaimed, fanning her face.

"Yeah. But even winter in California can regularly be really warm," Alexis said.

"Jerry must be dying," Kate mentioned. "He's wearing long sleeves."

Alex stood still. Suddenly she remembered a mystery she'd seen on TV. One where the bad guy had worn long sleeves in the middle of summer because the person he'd attacked had scratched his arms up, and he was trying to hide the wounds.

She told Kate about it.

"Sounds kind of scary," Kate said.

"It was, kind of. But they caught the bad guy in the end," Alexis said. "I don't think Jerry was bitten by an animatron he moved, or anything."

"Probably just protecting his arms from that smelly manure," Kate said. "Who wants that on your skin."

"Yeah," Alexis said. "But it's odd. I don't think I've ever seen him wear long sleeves—even in winter."

Alexis took out the water bottle again. The pink around the rim looked familiar, but she couldn't remember where she had seen it before. She glanced at Kate. Nope. Her Camp Club friend only wore lip balm. Maybe her mom? No. Mrs. Howell favored a mauve-colored lipstick. Oh well. It probably had nothing to do with the case, anyway. More than likely, it was just misplaced garbage, like Kate had said.

Alexis's good mood deflated like a punctured beach ball. They really didn't have anything to go on after all. *Maybe* they would see someone sneaking around the park with a rash creeping up his or her arm. *Maybe* the second suspect was a girl who liked pink lip gloss. Too many "maybes." Nothing was for sure.

Alexis couldn't help but think that maybe Miss Maria would be better off if the Camp Club Girls had stuck to investigating missing Spider Man socks.

An Unexpected Visitor

The girls were bummed out, to say the least. They walked back to the visitors' center and found Mrs. Smith bustling around like a caffeinated squirrel.

"She's been doing this all morning," said Megan as Alexis and Kate walked in. Megan was folding maps on the floor because Mrs. Smith's notes for the school board meeting were clogging up the desk.

"I hope you guys have been praying!" Mrs. Smith said as she searched for her paper clips. "This could be huge! If the school board approves my program, we won't have to worry about money. People will line up to donate!"

"That would be awesome, Mrs. Smith," said Alexis. "Are students allowed at this meeting?"

"Of course! Would you like to come? I can take you home when it's over."

"Yes!" said Alexis. She had never been to something as important as a meeting with the school board.

"Actually, since you go to one of the schools that

would be involved in the program, you could really help. If we can show that students are interested in the park, the board can't ignore us."

Alexis had just sat on the floor next to Megan, but she jumped up like she had sat on a cactus. She had an idea.

"Mrs. Smith?" she asked. "Would it help to have a lot of students at the meeting?"

"Sure," said Mrs. Smith. "But they would have to behave themselves. And they need to know why we're there. There will be a time where you guys will be allowed to speak if you want. If you invite anyone else, make sure they know what we're fighting for and why."

Alexis smiled. She grabbed Megan and Kate by the sleeves of their shirts.

"Come on!" she said, and pulled them out of the visitors' center without an explanation.

"What are we doing?" asked Megan. She was half running, half stumbling down the path after Alexis.

"We're going to your house!" said Alexis. "It's a lot closer than mine. You have last year's yearbook, right?" Megan nodded, out of breath. "Great!"

Minutes later they were at Megan's kitchen table with three Cokes, the yearbook, and a phone book. Kate was matching names in the yearbook to corresponding phone numbers. She was good at guessing. The names in the phone book were usually parents' names, but she had only given Alexis a few wrong numbers. The hardest one to find so far had been Kelli Jones. There were five pages of Joneses in the Sacramento area phone book.

As Kate gave Megan and Alexis phone numbers, the girls took turns calling. They left messages where they could, and when they talked to someone they told them to call all of their friends, too. Alexis hoped that this would help Mrs. Smith at the meeting tonight. If she could get twenty-five or thirty students to show up, they could really make an impact.

•—•—•

That night, when Mrs. Smith pulled up to the Department of Education, a huge group of teenagers was gathered on one side of the doors. Most of the students wore khakis and polo shirts, which made them look like miniature versions of their working parents. The rest of the students stood out in various blue and crimson uniforms, showing their school spirit.

The entire girls' volleyball team had left practice early to be there. So had most of the football team. Alexis got out of the car and straightened out her cheerleading skirt before going over to greet the crowd.

"Wow," said Mrs. Smith. "I never expected. . ."

"Don't worry, Mrs. Smith," said Kate. "You do your

128

thing. We have this totally under control."

The meeting room was short on seats, so many of the students sat in the aisles or stood against the walls. Alexis heard an adult mumble something about the fire marshal. He looked around the packed room, amazed.

The first half hour of the meeting was spent talking about budgets, bus routes, and banning tuna and pea casserole from the cafeteria. The students cheered when the board agreed to rework the cafeteria menus, but they settled down as the board director called Mrs. Smith's name. He was a tall, balding man with a kind face.

"Mrs. Smith, would you like to present your idea to the board? We have all read your detailed proposal, but an overview would be nice. There seem to be many people here to support you!" He smiled.

"Yes, Director Burgess. Thank you." Mrs. Smith stood up and took a deep breath. "I am here tonight as a representative from Aspen Heights Conservation Park. If you have seen the news at all lately, you will recognize our name."

As if on cue, Thad Swotter chose that exact moment to push his way into the room, followed by his cameraman. His ball cap was nowhere to be seen. Instead his bright hair was plastered in place, and his tie was as crazy as ever, though Alexis thought it looked a little loose. Mrs. Smith ignored the interruption. She cleared her throat and continued.

"Our park," she said, "consists of hundreds of acres of native Californian wildlife. There are many species of plant and trees that are common, like the mule ear or Jeffrey Pine, but we take pride in our wide selection of endangered plants as well. In some cases, Aspen Heights in the only place for hundreds of miles these plants can be found.

"This, along with how close the park is to Sacramento, makes it the perfect destination for field trips. It takes less than thirty minutes to get there from any school in the county, and the park appeals to many subjects. Biology and botany are two obvious choices, but the park has a great history as well. There are large stones with grooves where Native Americans used to grind their grains, as well as a stream that was panned for gold during the California Gold Rush in the 1800s.

"I propose a direct connection between our schools and Aspen Heights. We will give regular guided tours and educational walks for students of all ages."

Mrs. Smith finished and looked expectantly at the board.

"And how much would this 'partnership' cost us, Mrs. Smith?" asked Mimsy Button, the oldest woman on the board of education, and quite possibly the oldest woman in the Golden State altogether.

"One of my associates, Alexis Howell, has prepared to talk about that," said Mrs. Smith. "Alexis, would you like to step in?"

Alexis had been prepared to give part of Mrs. Smith's speech. Mrs. Smith told her the board would love hearing from a student, so even though she was nervous, she stood up and faced the board. She repeated a verse, Deuteronomy 31:6, to herself that Elizabeth had texted to her earlier, "Be strong and courageous. Do not be afraid or terrified because of them, for the Lord your God goes with you; he will never leave you nor forsake you."

"It won't cost the schools a dime, Mrs. Button," Alexis said with a shaky smile. "Just gas for the buses, of course."

"Well," said Mrs. Button, "that sounds too good to be true." She turned to Mrs. Smith. "If you don't mind my asking—what's in it for you?"

Mrs. Smith smiled and nodded. She wanted Alexis to keep going. Every eye in the room was pinned on her.

"First of all," she said, "Miss Maria built this park to teach our community. People come and go, but she wants to find a more permanent way to share her knowledge. This program would do that. Also, it would help the park get donations, so we could keep it looking good and keep giving free tours."

"Well," said Mr. Burgess, the board director, "this sounds wonderful. I would love to see this program take off."

The room was filled with the cheers of students. Mrs. Smith smiled and hugged Alexis hard.

"One more question," said Mrs. Button, who had all but shouted into her microphone. She silenced the cheering crowd with one raised, wrinkled hand. "I have *heard* that there might be controversial elements to your park."

"Controversial elements?" asked Mrs. Smith. Alexis didn't know what Mrs. Button meant, but it didn't sound good.

"Yes," said Mrs. Button. "Christian elements?"

Mrs. Smith threw a scathing look at Thad Swotter, whose face had drained of all color, except for a blotchy red area on his neck. He reached blindly behind him and covered the lens of the news camera.

"What do you mean?" asked Mrs. Smith, turning her attention back to the board at the front of the room.

"Miss Maria has scattered her Christian beliefs among the scientific facts of the park, has she not?" said Mrs. Button. "The place is littered with Bible verses."

"Is this true, Miss Ellena?" asked Mr. Burgess.

"No, there aren't any verses. We do have some plants

from the biblical regions, and we post some of their history."

"Why haven't you mentioned it before now?"

"To be honest, sir, I didn't think it mattered," Mrs. Smith said firmly. Alexis could see that she was trying to hide her anger.

"Sadly, it does matter. We can't be seen to promote one religion over the other. Surely you understand."

Now Alexis was getting upset.

"But sir," she said, "a historical fact about a plant doesn't promote—"

"I'm sorry, ladies. Please notify us if Miss Maria decides to remove these, um, Christian elements."

"Sir, she never will," said Mrs. Smith sadly. Alexis felt horrible. All of Mrs. Smith's hard work was slipping away.

"Then that is a loss for the community and our students," said the director. He banged his wooden hammer on the desk and the board filed out of the room. Mrs. Smith and Alexis were standing in the middle of the horde of students, mouths hanging open.

Thad Swotter waded his way over to them, pulling at his collar as if it were suddenly too hot.

"Mrs. Smith," he said. "I never meant to—"

"Leave me alone, Thad," Mrs. Smith said, yanking her arm out of his grasp. "I can't believe you would tell her those things!" Mrs. Smith stormed from the building.

Alexis thought Thad looked stunned, and a little sad. Maybe he hadn't done this on purpose, but did it matter? His big mouth had shut down the last chance they had to save the park! Thad turned to go, and Alexis saw him loosen his tie and undo the collar of his shirt. She stopped dead in her tracks.

An angry red rash stood out on the white skin of his neck like spilled tomato sauce on a ski slope. Thad Swotter had poison oak.

Alexis, Kate, Jerry, and Megan filed into the car. All of the other students were speeding off with their parents. No one said a word. They hung their heads, defeated.

Alexis was having a hard time holding back her tears. She kept blotting her stinging eyes on her skirt.

The park was back to square one. The poison oak told her that Thad Swotter probably *was* the one planting prints, but she didn't even care at the moment. In a few weeks, Miss Maria would have to return the dinosaurs, and then it wouldn't matter who was moving them around.

●—●—●

Twenty minutes later they pulled into Alexis's driveway. There weren't any words that would make everyone feel better, so she and Kate just waved good-bye. They mumbled a glum "hello" to Mr. Howell, who was watching a baseball game, and tromped up the stairs.

Alexis couldn't believe how things were turning out. How could stuff get so messed up when you're trying your hardest to make it right?

She had been working all week to solve the dinosaur mystery. She had walked miles around the park, spent her entire allowance, and lost a ton of sleep. And besides all of that, she had been praying all week. Praying that God would help her solve the mystery. Praying that God would provide for Miss Maria.

She was on her bed, eyes open, as if she could gaze through the ceiling and past the universe, right into God's office.

"Why won't You just fix things already?" she whispered.

Bling! Alexis looked over at her laptop. She had a new e-mail from Elizabeth, the oldest of the Camp Club Girls. After the meeting, she and Kate posted what had happened on the Camp Club Girls web page. All of the girls had sent back prayers and encouragement, but this was the message Alexis had been waiting for. Elizabeth always encouraged her, but for some reason she calmed Alexis more than anyone else. Maybe it was the Bible verses she always added to her advice.

> *Alex,*
>
> *Don't worry, but be strong and courageous because God is always with you (Joshua 1:9). Don't give up now—because we have God, we will always have hope (Jeremiah 29:11). And God works all things to the good of those who love him (Romans 8:28). The deal with the school might not have worked out, but I believe that He has something bigger and better in mind for Miss Maria. Keep investigating. When I am at my lowest is when the case usually breaks wide open! Love you! Tell Kate hi!*
>
> *Elizabeth*

Kate came into the bedroom. She had just taken a shower and was combing the tangles out of her sopping bob.

"Didn't you use a towel?" teased Alexis. "You're drenching my carpet!"

"You're in a better mood," said Kate. She smiled and tossed Alexis a Coke she had brought upstairs.

"Yeah," said Alexis, stretching out on the bed. "Elizabeth just wrote."

DING!

A clear, high-pitched note rang through the house.

"Was that the doorbell?" asked Kate.

"Yeah," said Alexis. She looked at the clock by her bed. It was nine o'clock. "Who would come to our house at this time of night?"

CHAPTER 11

The Visitor

Alexis and Kate were supposed to be getting ready for bed, but their curiosity got the better of them. The girls slipped out of the bedroom and tiptoed down the stairs. At the bottom, they stood behind a stack of paper and listened. The person outside gave up on the doorbell and began pounding instead. Whoever it was, they were in a hurry.

"Coming," called Mr. Howell. He was out of his chair, but he wasn't moving toward the door. His eyes were still glued to the ninth inning playing out on the television.

"Come *on*, Dad!" whispered Alexis. She didn't know why, but she felt sure that this late-night visitor was the answer to her prayers.

Mr. Howell opened the door, but it was in the way. Alexis couldn't see who was standing on the other side.

"Mr. Howell?" said a man's voice. Alexis couldn't place it, but it sounded familiar.

"Um, yes," said Mr. Howell. Alexis saw her dad stand

up on his tiptoes and peer past the visitor into the night.

"I'm alone, sir," said the man on the porch.

"Okay. If you're alone, then why are you here?"

Mr. Howell relaxed a little but crossed his arms. Alexis realized that this was a defensive stance, but her father wasn't scared. Without using words, her dad was saying, "Just try to get by me and see what happens."

Who was on the porch?

"Sir, your daughter has been investigating some strange things at Aspen Heights."

"Yes," said Mr. Howell. "I know. What does that have to do with you?"

"Well, I have some new information. After tonight, I am willing to do whatever it takes to help her."

"All right," said Mr. Howell. "I have to admit that this is more than a little strange. Come on in. I'll call Alexis down."

Mr. Howell moved back to let the visitor come inside, and Alexis gasped.

The porch light shone bright in the night, illuminating the yellow hair and crazy tie of Thad Swotter.

●—●—●

"I know you think I'm the bad guy, but just hear me out."

Thad Swotter was sitting on the edge of a squishy arm chair. Alexis and Kate stared at him from the couch, and

Alexis wished she hadn't left her notebook upstairs. Mr. Howell sat in his favorite chair, but he wasn't watching the TV anymore, even though the game had gone into extra innings. His eyes were locked on the nervous reporter.

"You know I've been sneaking into the park at night," said Swotter. "I told you that the other day. Like I said then, I've been taking pictures of the dinosaurs before anyone else could."

Alexis tapped the tips of her fingers on her knee. Biscuit trotted into the room and began to chew on the leg of her polka dot pajama pants.

"And?" she said. She had already heard all of this. Did he really have any new information to give her? And what if he wasn't telling the truth? Would he lie to make them think he was innocent?

Swotter smiled.

"Didn't you ever wonder how I knew the dinosaurs had been moved?" he asked.

"Well, yeah," said Alexis. "We thought you just checked the park every night."

"*Or*, of course, that you moved them yourself," said Kate. Her eyebrows arched above the bright green rims of her glasses. "And took your pictures afterward."

Alexis smiled. Like Kate had said the other day, you didn't just believe people were innocent because they said so. The Camp Club Girls had to follow the facts to get to the truth, and most of the facts still pointed to Thad Swotter.

"Is that poison oak, Mr. Swotter?" asked Mr. Howell. "It looks uncomfortable. Would you like something to put on it?"

"This?" said Thad, pointing to his neck. "It's not that bad." But he undid his tie, letting it hang loose around his neck.

"Oh! I forgot," squealed Alexis. "Whoever has been moving the dinosaurs covered up our camera the other night with a pile of leaves!"

Kate almost fell off the couch.

"That's right!" she said, straightening her glasses. "And the leaves we found today by the camera were poison oak!"

Thad opened his mouth, but Mr. Howell interrupted him.

"Can you explain all of this, Thad? There's a lot of evidence against you right now. I've seen my girl's notebook. Your shoes are the same as the criminal's. You've been sneaking around the park at night, and now this? Sounds like too many coincidences. . ."

"But they aren't coincidences!" said Swotter, smiling. "Don't you see? I've been tromping around the woods in the dark. I was bound to get poison oak sooner or later!

I think I got this the night you two followed me—had to pull some plants out of the way of my shot. Anyway, I'll stop talking. I have something else I want you to hear."

The reporter plunged his arm into his bag, and pulled out—

"Your cell phone?" said Alexis. "How's that going to help?"

"You aren't going to believe me until you hear it," said Swotter. He punched in a number and turned on the speaker phone. The mechanical voice of a woman echoed through the living room.

"Please enter your password," she said. Thad Swotter punched in four digits. "You have. . .*two*. . .saved messages. First. . .message."

The tinny voice of the woman was replaced by the scratchy sound of silence. After a few seconds, another voice spoke.

"Hello, Thad Swotter."

It sounded low and muffled, as if someone were speaking through a blanket or something.

"They're disguising their voice?" said Mr. Howell.

"Shh!" said Alexis, swatting a hand toward her father. The message continued.

"If you want the story of a lifetime, be at Aspen Heights at midnight. I'll leave directions for you on the

entrance sign." The line went dead, and the mechanical phone voice was back.

"Next saved message—" but Swotter turned it off.

"You see?" he said. "I'm not moving the dinosaurs. I've gotten a message every night this week. They tell me where to go to take my pictures. This was the first one."

Alexis and Kate were stunned. Mr. Howell leaned forward, curious.

"What kind of directions did they leave you, Mr. Swotter?" asked Alexis.

"Oh, I saved them. They're right here." He pulled a wrinkled note out of his bag. Alexis grabbed it. Her heart was pounding. The typing on the paper looked eerily familiar.

Mr. Swotter: the story you seek is on the move. Check out the park. . .see anything different?

"That was the first night, after Miss Maria got hurt," said Swotter. "After that, I didn't get any more notes— just the phone calls. I answered the phone a few times and tried to get more information, but the person always hangs up after they tell me where the dinosaurs are."

Alexis couldn't believe this. Her number-one suspect had walked into her living room with amazing evidence! Somehow she knew that Thad Swotter was telling the truth. He usually looked like he was hiding something, but tonight there was something different about his eyes. They weren't smiling, mocking Alexis and her investigation. They really looked concerned. Thad Swotter wanted to help.

"Okay," said Alexis slowly. "So it isn't you, but how will this tell us who it *is*?" Swotter opened his mouth, but Kate was faster.

"The phone numbers!" she said. "Cell phones keep track of who has called! It lists their phone numbers until you decide to delete them." She looked at the reporter, her eyes huge behind her glasses. "Please tell me you didn't delete them!"

"Of course not!" he said. "That's the best part." He pushed a few buttons, scrolling down a list of phone numbers. Alexis couldn't believe her luck. If they got the phone number of whoever was doing this, they might be able to figure out who it was. They could call the number and see who answered, and if that didn't work they could get online. She saw her mom find the name of a prank caller one time by putting in the phone number—like a backward phone book.

"Here it is," said Swotter. "This is the number that came up all week." He turned the phone around so everyone could see. Mr. Howell had been sucked in and was now squished next to the girls on the couch.

"Unavailable?" he said. "How does that help?"

"It doesn't," said Kate. But the reporter informer was scrolling through more numbers.

"I said that was the number that came up all week," he said. "All week, that is, except last night. Last night, the caller got messy and used a landline—a regular phone—instead of a blocked cell phone. Look." He spun the phone around again, and ten digits lit up the screen.

"Do you know whose number that is?" asked Kate in a whisper.

"Nope," said Swotter. "I thought I'd save that for you guys." He handed the phone to Alexis, who looked at her dad. He nodded, and she pressed SEND.

Somewhere, miles away, a phone was ringing. The echo of it came through the tiny speaker of Thad Swotter's flip phone. After the fourth ring, an answering machine picked up.

"Hello, you have reached Aspen Heights Conservation Park. We are not available to—"

The phone slid out of Alexis's hand and snapped closed as it hit the floor.

●—●—●

Thad Swotter picked up his phone and glanced at the time flashing on the front of it.

"I hate to run, but I have some work to do," he said.

"I'll be at the park this weekend. Will you girls keep me updated?"

Alexis nodded. She was still a little shocked. The phone call came from Aspen Heights. Had someone broken into the visitors' center to use the phone? That had to be it. Nothing else made sense.

Another thought struck her as they walked Mr. Swotter to the door.

"Mr. Swotter, why do you want to help us all of a sudden?"

"Well, really I wanted to help Mrs. Smith. This park means the world to her." Alexis looked confused, so Thad Swotter continued. "We were friends when we were kids, Mrs. Smith and I. Then we grew up and I—well—I forgot what it meant to be a friend. I put everything I had into becoming the best, and I hurt a few people along the way."

Thad Swotter apologized to Mr. Howell for intruding so late at night, and then walked back to his car with his hands in his pockets.

"Bedtime, ladies," said Mr. Howell. He laid his large hands on Alexis's shoulders and squeezed. "A lot of new stuff to think about, huh?"

"Yeah," said Alexis. She knew sleep would not come easy tonight. The girls went back upstairs and brushed their teeth. Five minutes later they were sitting cross-legged on the bed talking about who could have made the mysterious phone call.

"Someone must have broken into the center, Alex," said Kate. "That's the only thing that makes sense."

"I know," said Alexis. "Maria was in the hospital most of the week, so she couldn't have been moving the dinosaurs."

"She would never do that anyway, would she?"

"No," said Alexis. "No one at the park would do anything to put it in danger. We all love it too much." Alexis's excitement was deflating by the second. What good would this new evidence be if they couldn't find out *who* had made those calls?

"Hey, do you mind if I read Elizabeth's e-mail?" asked Kate.

"Go ahead," said Alexis. "Just open my mail box."

Kate walked over to the computer. It had gone into sleep mode, so she wiggled a finger over the touchpad to clear the black screen.

"Oh no!" she said. "Jerry forgot to take the camera down!" Alexis looked over at her computer. Sure enough, the camera was still in the tree. She hoped that nothing happened to it before they could take it down in the morning.

"It's still on," said Kate. "See the Raptors?"

"It must have gotten bumped," said Alexis. "It's sideways now."

"Yeah, it's kind of—" but Kate never finished her sentence.

"Kind of what?" Kate didn't answer, so Alexis sat up to get a better look at the video. "No way! Did you see who that was?"

Kate nodded, her mouth hanging open and her eyes glued to the screen.

The dinosaur movers were back, and they had forgotten all about the hidden camera.

CHAPTER 12

Good Intentions

Alexis's mind was racing. They had hardly slept because of their discovery. As soon as Mrs. Howell was up and about the girls were begging her to take them to the park.

"I knew I had seen that lip gloss before!"

How could she not have seen this coming? First the shoes—she had never really looked at his shoes, but now she remembered that he always wore Converse when he worked. And the lip gloss? It had been a gift *from Alexis*! How could she have forgotten that?

"It was you!"

Alexis stood over Jerry with her arms crossed. He was knee-deep in a hole he had dug for a new sapling.

"What do you mean?" Jerry said. He blushed and a crooked smile bloomed on his face. *Does he think this is a game?* Alexis wondered.

"I mean it was you moving the dinosaurs and placing the prints. You and Megan!"

Jerry laughed. "Prove it."

"First of all, your shoes." Alexis pointed at Jerry's feet, which were indeed soled with Converse All-Stars. "You got sloppy and started leaving your footprints everywhere. I don't know *how* I forgot that you wear those old things when you're going to get muddy."

"Lots of people wear these shoes, Alex," said Jerry. She could tell he was enjoying this.

"Sure. But you're wearing long sleeves again today, Jerry. Why?" Jerry squirmed a little. "Raise up your sleeve, if you don't mind."

Jerry pulled his shirt sleeve up to his elbow, revealing a nasty case of poison oak rash.

"You didn't realize what plant you used to cover the camera the other night, did you? Kate and I found wilted poison oak at the scene. And speaking of that scene. . ."

Alexis stomped past him to the tool shed. Yesterday he had kept her out of it. He said it was a mess. Jerry climbed out of the hole he was digging and followed her.

"No, you can't—" said Jerry, but he was too late. Alexis ripped the door open, flooding the small building with light.

"Ha!" she said. There, in the middle of the floor, was a pile of strange-looking tools. On closer inspection, the girls realized that they were long handles, like broom sticks, with wooden dinosaur feet screwed onto the bottoms. There were two pairs of them. Kate picked one up and noticed thin lines running up and down the foot.

"Those little lines we kept seeing in the tracks—it was the grain of the wood!" she said.

"Cool, huh?" asked Jerry.

Alexis was surprised. She had expected a confession, followed by an apology full of guilt. Instead, Jerry stepped past her into the shed with a huge smile on his face.

"I figured you would catch on sooner or later," Jerry said. "Watch this!" He pulled out the largest pair of wooden feet—Alexis assumed they belonged to the Tyrannosaurus Rex—and stood on them, holding onto the wooden handles at the top. Then he began walking around on them like a pair of stilts.

"See?" he said. "Cool, huh? I thought all this up!" He grinned. Did he expect her to be proud of him? So Bailey had been right after all!

"This isn't a game, Jerry!" Alexis said. "People could have been hurt!"

"Well, no one was," he said. He jumped off the wooden feet and tossed them back into the shed. "Miss Maria needed people to show up. I was saving the park."

"What's wrong?" Megan asked as she walked up behind Alexis and Kate.

"Look, Kate," said Alexis, pointing to Megan. "It's our

Lip Gloss Lady." She turned to Megan to explain. "We found a water bottle with your lip gloss all over it in a bush near the Raptors."

Megan looked confused.

"Alexis and Kate finally caught us," Jerry explained. He still sounded as if the whole thing was hilarious. Megan, on the other hand, looked guilty. She stared at her feet and said, "Oh."

Alexis and Kate were staring at Jerry, waiting for an explanation.

"Come on, Alexis!" he said. "You know this place needs help! Thad Swotter gave me the idea, although he doesn't know it. He said in his newscast that this place needed a lot more than toy dinosaurs, and I agreed. You've seen how many people have been coming!"

"Yeah, but that doesn't fix the problem, Jerry!" said Alexis. "When the dinosaurs have to go back, what are you going to do then? They won't bring in any visitors once they're gone, no matter how 'alive' they were while they were here!"

Jerry wasn't smiling anymore. He strode into the shed and pulled a small object off a shelf. He handed it to Kate.

"My camera!" she squealed, delighted to have it back.

"Yeah," said Jerry. "We took it from your camp the

other night so you wouldn't see that it was us."

"That's stealing, Jerry!" said Alexis.

"Not really! We were going to give it back!" Jerry stood looking moodily at Alexis until they were interrupted by a familiar figure limping with a crutch under one arm.

"Miss Maria!" they all yelled at once. The group rushed forward to hug her but stopped short so they wouldn't hurt her.

"I trust my park is in one piece?" Miss Maria asked playfully. Then she noticed the tension in the group. "Now what's happened to make everyone so glum?"

"We found out who's been moving the dinosaurs and leaving the prints," said Alexis.

"Oh, that's wonderful!" said Miss Maria. "I knew I could count on you girls!"

"It was Jerry," Alexis said, and Miss Maria's smile disappeared.

"And me," said Megan. "I helped him."

"Well, that *is* a surprise," said Miss Maria. She looked severely disappointed.

"I don't see what the big deal is!" cried Jerry. "It got more people into the park! I was careful! None of the dinosaurs—or *people*," he looked pointedly at Alexis, "have been hurt!"

"You're right, Jerry," said Maria. "But that's not the main point. You were being deceitful. You pretended to help us when in fact you were the problem. If you came up with this idea, you should have just asked me if you could carry it out."

"I was afraid you would say no," Jerry said.

"And you were probably right," said Maria. "I don't want to trick people into loving my park. I want them to enjoy it for the same reasons I do."

"But they don't," said Jerry. "That's the problem! We're going to have to close the park!"

There were tears in his eyes now, and Alexis wondered if all of his joking had just been a cover-up for his real feelings. He was scared of losing the park—of losing his home. She reached out and grasped his hand, which was dirty and hot.

"God will take care of us," said Maria. "You'll see. He's got a way of showing up just when we need Him."

"That's the thing," said Jerry. "We've needed Him for a long time, and you've been praying nonstop. *I've* been praying nonstop!" Jerry pulled away from Alexis's hand and gestured around them. "In case you haven't noticed, He hasn't shown up yet."

Through the open window of the visitors' center, they heard the phone ring.

•—•—•

TO: Camp Club Girls
SUBJECT: Another one solved!

To my Camp Club Sisters,

Thanks for your prayers! The park is going to be okay! Miss Maria got a phone call yesterday from a company who wants to help us. They can't give her the money she needs outright, but they want to sponsor and promote a yearly 5K race through the park! They are going to provide prize bags for participants and help us with volunteers. Their spokesperson says that the race should raise enough money to help Miss Maria maintain the park, and maybe even expand it! We're planning to do the first race in October, when the aspens are golden for the fall! The park will be beautiful!

Some of the local teachers have called, too. They want to come to the park for field trips, even though Mrs. Smith's program isn't in place. They say that at first they'll avoid the greenhouse, which has the "Christian Elements" the board of directors didn't like. All except for Mr. Chase, the religion teacher at our local community college. He got all excited when he heard about the thorns. He said something

155

about persecution and Roman torture. . .eew.

But the best part is that all of the teachers told Miss Maria that they want to pay her a small fee for guided tours!

Thanks bunches to all of you for putting your heads together on this one! The "criminals" (my friend Jerry and his sister, Megan) realize the mistake they made. I think Jerry also learned a little something about God's faithfulness. Thanks, Elizabeth, for sending those Bible verses. I showed them to Jerry and he agrees that God always provides, even if it's not in the way or the timing we expect!

Love you all, and keep your eyes open! You never know who will need us next!

Alexis

Kate had flown home at the end of the week. Alexis was back at the park, kneeling in the dirt and planting flowers around a new sign at the head of the park trail. Next to her stood Jogger, who Miss Maria had decided to buy instead of returning him with the other dinosaurs. She said she could afford one of the smaller ones. Since they had all grown so close to the little Raptor, he was the obvious choice. His picture was all over the new brochures, and he was even going to be on some T-shirts they were going to sell in the visitors' center. He had become the perfect mascot.

Alexis had even come up with a great idea for the kids who visited the park. She drew a map and put a cartoon drawing of Jogger in the corner. The top read "Where's Jogger?" Each time kids came, they would get a map. The goal was to roam all over the park until they found Jogger and marked him on their map. When they had visited the park and found him four times they would get a prize.

Alexis couldn't help but think about the movie she and Kate had seen. The person they thought was so good ended up being the bad guy. It wasn't too far from what had happened here. She thought Thad Swotter was making trouble because he *seemed* like the kind of person who would. At the same time, she hadn't even thought of Jerry or Megan.

She had learned a lot about judging people before she really got to know them. Thad Swotter had ended up helping her, and she found out he could be a pretty nice guy.

At that moment, as Alexis pressed pink impatiens into the dirt, Thad Swotter walked up behind her.

"Is Mrs. Smith here?" he asked. "She's giving me a tour of the greenhouse."

"The greenhouse?" said Alexis. "But that's where—"

"I know, I know," he said, holding up a hand so he could explain.

"I've never really been interested in where things came from," Swotter said. "You know, creation versus monkeys and all that. But I think the reporter in me is taking over. For some reason, I can't stand not *knowing*. Besides, you guys weren't going to change things around here, no matter what the school board told you. I figure that if you're not willing to compromise, even with everything to lose, this God of yours must be pretty special."

Alexis was awestruck. Was this reporter—the man who would do anything for a story—actually saying he was interested in *God*?

"Mrs. Smith's in the visitors' center," she said. He thanked her and turned away.

"Oh, Mr. Swotter?" said Alexis. He stopped and looked back.

"Yes?"

"I'm sorry we blamed you for moving the dinosaurs and stuff," Alexis said.

"That's okay. You were just following your leads, and I shouldn't have been sneaking around the park in the dark anyway. That wasn't very honest of me." He stuck out his hand. "Call us even?"

Alexis shook it. "Even," she said. Swotter left and entered the visitors' center.

God was amazing, Alexis knew. He had helped her solve her mystery, provided for the park, and drawn Thad Swotter to Him all at once!

Alexis finished planting her flowers and stood to admire the effect. The new wooden sign glinted in the sun. The message on it had been her idea, and it made her laugh each time she read it:

PLEASE NO WALKING, JOGGING, RUNNING, LEAPING, TRAIPSING, MEANDERING, WANDERING, JUMPING, DRIFTING, HOPPING, STROLLING, SAUNTERING, AMBLING, MARCHING, STRIDING, PACING, HIKING, TODDLING, SPRINTING, LOPING, SCUTTLING, SCAMPERING, DARTING, DASHING, SCURRYING, BOUNDING, OR SKIPPING BEYOND THE PATH! THANK YOU!

Jogger the Raptor wagged his tail and smiled right along with her.

If you enjoyed

ALEXIS AND THE
SACRAMENTO SURPRISE

be sure to read other

CAMP CLUB GIRLS

books from BARBOUR PUBLISHING

Book 1: Mystery at Discovery Lake
Six girls meet at Camp Discovery and learn
they all share one thing in common: an apti-
tude for intrigue! They're soon emboriled in
a search for lost jewels.

ISBN 978-1-60260-267-0

Book 2: Sydney's DC Discovery
Sydney and Elizabeth are on-site in the
nation's capital when odd happenings oc-
cure at the Vietnam Memorial. Can they
decipher the clues and save the president
before the dawn's early light?

ISBN 978-1-60260-268-7

Book 3: McKenzie's Montana Mystery
When Bailey and McKenzie arrive to help at a
horse ranch in Montana, they're immediately
entrenched in mysteries. Can the Camp Club
Girls help Bailey and McKenzie save the
ranch?

ISBN 978-1-60260-269-4

AVAILABLE WHEREVER BOOKS ARE SOLD.